n

he
he

n't
lp
n
he
id
f?

Please return on or before the latest date above.
You can renew online at www.kent.gov.uk/libs
or by phone 08458 247 200

CUSTOMER SERVICE EXCELLENCE

Libraries & Archives

Kent
County
Council

Also by Lucy Daniels

TV Tie-in titles
Jess the Border Collie 1: The Arrival
Jess the Border Collie 2: The Challenge
Jess the Border Collie 3: The Runaway

Animal Ark Classics

Kittens in the Kitchen
Pony in the Porch
Dolphin in the Deep
Bunnies in the Bathroom
Puppies in the Pantry
Hamster in a Hamper
Horse in the House
Badger in the Basement
Cub in the Cupboard
Guinea-Pig in the Garage
Puppy in a Puddle
Hedgehogs in the Hall
Lamb in the Laundry
Foals in the Field
Koalas in a Crisis

With a special foreword from Lucy Daniels

For a full list of available Animal Ark titles,
see www.madaboutbooks.com

The Border Collie

LUCY DANIELS

Hodder
Children's
Books

A division of Hachette Children's Books

Special thanks to Helen Magee

Text copyright © 1998 Ben M. Baglio
Created by Ben M. Baglio, London W12 7QY
Illustrations copyright © 1998 Trevor Parkin

First published in Great Britain in 1998
by Hodder Children's Books
This edition published in 2005

2

A Catalogue record for this book is available
from the British Library

ISBN-10: 0 340 91710 5
ISBN-13: 9780340917107

Typeset in Bembo by Avon DataSet Ltd, Bidford on Avon, Warwickshire

Printed and bound in Great Britain by Bookmarque Ltd, Croydon, Surrey

The paper and board used in this paperback by Hodder Children's Books
are natural recyclable products made from wood grown in sustainable
forests. The manufacturing processes conform to the environmental
regulations of the country of origin.

Hodder Children's Books
a division of Hachette Children's Books
338 Euston Road
London NW1 3BH

1

'Stay, Jess,' Jenny Miles commanded, trying to sound severe.

Jess, her black-and-white Border collie, looked up at her pleadingly, his head to one side. Six months old now, Jess looked just as appealing as he had done when he was a tiny puppy. He had four white socks and a white chest and muzzle. The rest of him was coal black.

'Don't look at me like that,' Jenny said firmly as she shut the farm gate. 'You know you can't come to school with me.'

Jess put his two front paws on the bottom bar of the gate and howled.

'Oh, Jess,' Jenny said, giving his ears a rub. 'I'll miss you too but it's not long till the summer holidays. Then we'll have *weeks* together. And Matt will be home for the summer too.' Matt was Jenny's brother. He was now nineteen and away at agricultural college.

'Don't you worry about Jess, Jenny,' Mrs Grace reassured her. Ellen Grace was the housekeeper at Windy Hill Farm. 'He'll be fine once you're out of sight,' she continued. 'He always is.'

Jenny looked into Ellen Grace's warm blue eyes and smiled gratefully. 'You aren't just saying that are you, Mrs Grace?' she asked anxiously. 'I hate leaving him behind.'

Mrs Grace smiled. 'Jess knows that,' she said reassuringly. 'He just keeps hoping one day you'll take him with you. Once you've gone he settles down.'

Jenny bent once more and stroked Jess's soft

coat. 'Be good,' she whispered. 'I'll be back this afternoon.'

'And Jess will be waiting for you as usual,' Ellen Grace said.

Jenny gave Jess a final pat then jumped on her bicycle and pedalled off, turning at the bend in the farm track to wave once more.

Jess gave a last howl before he was lost to sight. Jenny sighed as she pedalled down the track. She didn't think she would ever get used to leaving Jess behind, but Mrs Grace wouldn't lie to her. Ellen Grace had been housekeeper at Windy Hill for nearly five months now and she loved Jess almost as much as Jenny did.

Windy Hill, she thought, as the breeze blew strands of hair over her face. The Mileses' farm was certainly well named. If she turned her head she could see up towards Darktarn Keep. It stood on a hill above the farm, its rugged outline softened by the sunshine.

Jenny slewed her bike to a stop halfway along the track. Here, the track followed the boundary fence of the farm's top field. Her father, a tall man with dark hair, walked across the field towards her with Nell and Jake, his two Border collies, at his heels. Around him, the flock of Blackface sheep bleated and bumped one another, parting before him. The lambs scrambled after their mothers, their little black faces looking comical against the soft white wool of their coats.

Jenny waved. 'Hi, Dad!' she called. She looked beyond Fraser Miles to where two young men were rounding up sheep. Her father had hired extra help for the sheep dipping.

'Morning, lass,' her father called back. 'How's Jess today?'

Fraser Miles reached the fence and leaned on a post. Beside him, Nell and Jake crouched low, waiting obediently for his next command. Jenny leaned over the fence and gave each of them a pat. Nell and Jake were Jess's parents.

'Just the same,' Jenny said. 'I think he'd rather be out with you and the sheep than having to stay at home.'

Fraser Miles smiled. 'He was a good help with the lambing,' he agreed.

Jess had been wonderful during the lambing earlier in the year. Jenny had strapped bottles of milk to a harness for him and he had managed to feed lots of lambs. The poor little things might have died otherwise.

'But he is a house dog, Jenny,' her father continued.

Jenny nodded. 'I know – and I'd much rather have him as a pet,' she agreed. 'How's the dipping going?'

Fraser Miles looked up at the sky. 'Fine! The weather couldn't be better for it,' he said. 'Sunshine and a south wind.'

Jenny knew that sheep dipping was best carried out in fine weather when the fleeces got a chance to dry off afterwards. 'Will you get them all done in time?' she asked.

'If the weather holds for another few days,' her father replied. 'We start shearing next month.'

'Matt will be home to give you a hand by then,' Jenny said, smiling. She was looking forward to having her brother home for the holidays.

'I'll certainly need his help,' Fraser Miles replied. 'Shearing nearly a thousand sheep is a big job.'

'You'll manage, Dad,' Jenny said encouragingly. 'You always do.'

Mr Miles laughed and ruffled his daughter's hair. 'With that vote of confidence how can I fail?' he said. 'Have a good day at school, lass.'

Jenny pulled a face. 'OK, I'm going. I can take a hint,' she said. 'See you later, Dad.'

Mr Miles turned away and whistled to his dogs. Nell and Jake sprang up, alert to his commands. Jenny watched them racing along the edge of the flock, gathering together the ewes her father had selected for dipping. Mr Miles and his helpers would dip them in batches in the swimbath.

Jenny stood where she was for a few minutes, admiring the sheepdogs as they worked. Blackfaces were a skittish breed and it took a good dog to manage them. But Nell and Jake were doing fine. Jenny watched Jake. He seemed to have made a complete recovery. During lambing he'd become entangled with some barbed wire and very nearly bled to death. But now he was back out in the fields with Nell, as though it had never happened. They really *were* the best working dogs in the Borders.

Reluctantly, she turned away and pushed her bike off. She would much rather have stayed and watched – or, better still, helped!

Jenny pedalled on towards the road that led to the large village of Graston nearby. The wind whipped her honey-brown hair out behind her as she crested the hill that ran down to Graston School. She could see Graston village laid out below her. The village nestled in a valley, surrounded by farmland. The bell-tower of the little church rose above the roofs of the houses. The school was at the edge of the village and its pupils came not only from Graston itself, but also from the surrounding farms and the fishing village of Cliffbay, on the nearby coast. To the east of the village the sea sparkled in the summer sunshine.

Jenny freewheeled the last stretch of hill down to Graston and turned in at the school gates just as a bright orange Mini with a sunflower painted on the roof drew up.

'Hi, Jenny!' Carrie Turner, Jenny's best friend, leaped out of the passenger seat of the car almost before it had stopped.

Jenny waved. 'Hi, Carrie. Hi, Mrs Turner.'

Mrs Turner smiled at Jenny, tooted the car horn in reply and sped off, looking just as cheerful as the sunflower on the car roof. The Turners lived in Cliffbay, in a house right next to the sea. Mr Turner ran boat trips from the harbour there. Mrs Turner often dropped Carrie off at school, but Carrie could easily walk home: it was only a mile or so – and downhill all the way.

'Mum's in a hurry this morning,' Carrie explained. 'She's teaching a painting class in Greybridge and she's late already.'

Mrs Turner was an artist. She had painted a picture of Jess that had been used in a national fundraising campaign in aid of animal welfare. Jenny had a framed copy of the illustration on her bedroom wall.

'So what's new?' Jenny grinned at Carrie. 'Your mum's always running late. It must be the artistic temperament.'

Carrie grinned back. Like her mother, she had red hair and a dusting of freckles across her nose.

'How was Jess this morning?' Carrie asked, slinging her schoolbag carelessly over her shoulder.

'Watch out, Carrie!' said a boy coming in at the gate behind her.

'Oops, sorry, Ian,' Carrie apologised, whirling round, her schoolbag flying again. Jenny ducked and Ian Amery gave her a grin.

'You've been practising avoiding that school-bag,' he said.

Jenny nodded. Ian was Mrs Grace's nephew. He was staying with his aunt while his parents set up home in Canada.

'Carrie's schoolbag is lethal,' Jenny replied, smiling.

Carrie turned up her nose. 'It's all the heavy books I have to carry,' she explained. 'Anyway, how is Jess?'

'Still howling,' Jenny sighed. 'He's been like this ever since I went back to school after the Easter holidays. He got so used to me being around that he can't understand why I keep going away now.'

'He probably misses working with the sheep too,' Ian said.

Jenny nodded. 'Poor Jess,' she sighed again. 'He looks so miserable when I leave him behind.'

Ian looked sympathetic but Carrie's attention was distracted. 'There's somebody else who looks miserable,' she said, pointing across the playground. 'I wonder what's wrong with Paul.'

Jenny looked over to where Carrie was pointing. A small boy was standing in the far corner by himself, feet scuffing the ground, head down.

'That isn't like Paul,' Carrie said, concerned. 'He's usually running around, playing.'

Paul McLay was seven years old and the son of the farmer who owned Dunraven, the farm next to Windy Hill. Calum McLay and Jenny's dad didn't get on with each other and Paul's older sister, Fiona, was always being spiteful. But Paul was quite different – much nicer than his father and sister.

'Maybe we'd better see if he's all right,' said Carrie.

'You go, Jenny,' Ian suggested. 'Paul likes you and you're really tactful – usually!'

Jenny flushed. She and Ian had had a blazing row the first time they had met. They were still just a little wary of each other.

'Ian's right,' said Carrie. 'You go and talk to Paul.'

Jenny made her way across to the little boy. She made sure that he could see her before she started speaking. Paul had been deaf since he was four when he'd suffered a viral infection which had affected his hearing. But he could now lip-read very well indeed, if you spoke directly to him. 'Hi, Paul! Is anything the matter?' Jenny asked, as she approached him.

Paul's wide grey eyes looked sadly up at her, and he nodded. He really did seem miserable.

'What is it?' Jenny asked.

Paul's lip trembled and he drew a hand across his eyes. 'Mum and Dad want me to go into hospital,' he said, his voice unsteady. 'I'm supposed to have an operation on my ears.'

Jenny frowned. 'What's the operation for?' she asked. Then her face brightened. 'Will it bring your hearing back?'

Paul shrugged. 'It *might*,' he replied. 'But I don't want to go. I'm scared,' he confessed.

'Have you told your mum and dad you're scared?' Jenny asked.

Paul nodded. 'I told Mum,' he replied. 'The

last time I was in hospital, it hurt.'

Jenny looked at him sympathetically. 'Ears *are* painful when they get infected,' she agreed. 'But maybe it won't hurt so much this time.'

Paul stared down at his feet, his hair hanging over his eyes. 'It will,' he murmured.

Jenny touched his arm and he looked at her. She drew in her breath at the sadness in his eyes. It reminded her of Jess when she left him each morning to go to school.

'Jess had to have an operation to fix his leg,' she told Paul. 'It wasn't very easy for him but he can run around much better now. He was really brave about it.' Jess had been born with a twisted leg and had needed to spend weeks in a cast to set it straight.

'I'm not brave,' Paul said, his eyes filling with tears.

Jenny took a deep breath. 'It's all right to be frightened, Paul,' she said. 'I was scared when Jess had his operation. Being frightened doesn't mean you aren't brave.'

Paul still didn't say anything, but Jenny could tell he was thinking hard about what she was saying. She went on speaking. 'Sometimes, when I'm feeling sad or upset, I go to Darktarn Keep. That's my favourite place. My mum used to take me there a lot when I was your age. She told me all sorts of stories about the Border reivers who used to live around Graston.'

'Your mum died, didn't she?' Paul asked.

Jenny felt a sharp pang. A whole year had passed since her mother's death, but it still wasn't easy to talk about it. 'Yes,' she said softly. 'She died in a riding accident last summer.'

'Is that why you get sad and go to the keep?' Paul asked.

Jenny nodded. 'And when I get upset about anything else it really helps to go to my favourite place. Do *you* have a favourite place?'

Paul shook his head. He looked so downcast, Jenny's heart went out to him. She had an idea. 'Would you like to come to Windy Hill and visit Jess?' she suggested. 'Then you could see how well he's done since having his operation.'

Paul's face lit up. 'I'd like that,' he said. Then his face fell. 'But Dad won't let me come to Windy Hill. He doesn't like your dad.'

Jenny sighed. Paul was right. Mr McLay didn't like Fraser Miles. He wouldn't let Paul

14

come to Windy Hill. Many years earlier, before Jenny's parents had married, Jenny's mother, Sheena, was to marry Calum McLay. But at the last moment, Sheena had changed her mind and married Fraser Miles instead. Calum had been furious at losing both Sheena and her farm, Windy Hill, to Fraser. He had wanted revenge on Fraser ever since, by trying to take Windy Hill Farm away from him.

'Maybe we could meet at the keep,' Jenny suggested to Paul. 'You know where it is, don't you? It's near the little lake above our farm.'

Paul nodded. 'Ian took me bird-watching at that lake once,' he said. 'Only he called it a tarn.'

'Lakes like that are called tarns in the Borders,' Jenny smiled. 'Ian was quite right. I could bring Jess there. That would be OK, wouldn't it?'

Paul looked eagerly at her, his face brightening. 'When?' he asked.

'Saturday afternoon,' Jenny said decisively. 'Two o'clock. Will that be all right?'

Paul nodded. 'I'll bring my new binoculars,' he said. 'I can look at the birds on the tarn.'

Paul was a very keen bird-watcher and the lake below the keep was a great place for divers and ducks.

Jenny smiled in relief. Paul's face had lost almost all of its sadness now. 'It's a date, Paul,' she said.

'Saturday,' Paul repeated, smiling up at her. 'And don't forget Jess.'

Jenny smiled. 'I could *never* forget Jess,' she said.

2

Jenny shivered slightly as she and Jess waited
for Paul the following Saturday. The weather
had been good all week but now it looked as if
it had taken a turn for the worse. Dark clouds
were beginning to mass out to sea. Jess barked,
drawing her attention to Paul as the little boy
appeared, walking towards Darktarn Keep.
Jenny waved at Paul from her perch on one of
the broken walls of the keep.

Paul waved back and Jenny bent to Jess. 'Go and show him the way, Jess,' she whispered in the collie's ear. 'Go and get Paul!'

Jess gave a short bark and raced off down the slope of the hill towards Paul. Jenny watched as her dog wended his way round the fallen rock and long grass at the base of the keep. He scampered towards the drystone wall that bordered the field beyond, scrambled over it and darted under the weathered trunk of a fallen tree, making straight for Paul.

Jenny's eyes rested on the fallen tree for a moment. That was where Sheena Miles, Jenny's mother, had been killed last year. Her father had told her how her mother had been out riding when a sudden storm blew up. Lightning had struck the tree, forcing her mother to pull Mercury up in order to avoid it. Then her mother had been thrown from the horse and had died. Jenny gazed at the tree, feeling a swift pang of grief at the thought of her mother's death.

She lifted her head as a sudden wind blew up, letting it stream through her hair. Her mother had always loved this place. Darktarn

Keep stood on top of a rise above Windy Hill. It was a ruin now, its broken tower jutting upwards, dark against the sky, but the view was magnificent.

From here, Jenny could look out over her father's fields stretching right down to the cliffs that bordered the sea. She could see Puffin Island, a bird sanctuary, gleaming in the sun as the heavy clouds parted for a moment. Gulls wheeled round its low, rocky headland.

Jenny turned as she heard Paul cry out delightedly. Jess had reached the little boy and was running round him, barking a welcome. She smiled. Jess's twisted leg was almost straight now and most people would never guess there had ever been anything wrong with it.

Paul bent to the collie and ruffled the young dog's ears in greeting while Jess leaped up, almost knocking Paul over in his eagerness to welcome him. Jenny heard Paul laugh as the collie ran a few paces forward and looked back. Jess never barked at Paul, seeming to know that Paul couldn't hear him.

'OK, I'm coming,' Paul called to Jess.

Then boy and dog made their way up

through the fallen rocks to the place where Jenny was sitting.

'Wow!' said Paul as they arrived. 'I've never been up here before. This is great.'

'It used to be a stronghold for the Border reivers,' Jenny explained, turning to Paul as he plonked himself down beside her.

'What are reivers?' Paul asked.

'Robbers,' Jenny told him. 'I used to come up here with Mum when I was little. She told me loads of stories about the reivers – how they used to steal each other's sheep in the olden days.'

'That must have been really exciting,' Paul said, his hand on Jess's neck.

Jess lay contentedly between them, his pink tongue hanging out. Jenny nodded. 'Dangerous too, I should think,' she agreed. 'I love it up here. Look, you can see Puffin Island.'

Paul undid the case of his binoculars and raised them to his eyes. 'Wow!' he said. 'I can see kittiwakes nesting on the cliffs out there.'

'Those must be really good binoculars,' Jenny laughed.

'They are,' agreed Paul. 'Mum gave them to

me because I was upset about going into hospital.'

'Are you still worried?' she asked.

Paul sighed heavily. 'I don't want to go,' he replied. He looked away from her, fiddling with the strap on his binoculars. 'The doctor puts you to sleep,' he said.

Jenny touched his arm and he turned back to her. 'That's so that the operation doesn't hurt,' she told him. 'You go to sleep, then when you wake up it's all over.'

Paul swallowed and his lower lip trembled.

'What is it, Paul?' Jenny asked. 'What are you *really* worried about?'

Paul gulped. 'What if I don't wake up?' he asked in a small voice.

Jenny gasped. 'But of course you will,' she said.

'Fiona says sometimes people *don't* wake up,' he said. 'They just sleep and sleep for ever!'

Jenny looked at him, shocked. Fiona was Paul's elder sister. 'Has Fiona been scaring you?' she asked, hardly able to believe it.

Paul hung his head but didn't answer. Jenny felt anger rising in her. How dare Fiona scare her own little brother like this!

Paul stretched out a hand to Jess. The puppy came and laid his head in Paul's lap. Paul buried his fingers in Jess's soft fur.

Jenny looked at Paul with concern. The little boy was clearly struggling against tears. 'I don't think you should listen to Fiona,' she told him. 'Why don't you talk to your mum and dad about it? If you really don't want to go to hospital they wouldn't make you.'

'Dad wants me to go,' Paul confided. He swallowed hard. 'I don't think Dad likes me being deaf,' he said softly.

Jenny sighed. This was very difficult. 'I'm sure he'd rather you were able to hear – for *your* sake,' she said, looking into Paul's troubled eyes. 'But that doesn't mean he or your mum would want you to be unhappy – or that they love you any less for being deaf.'

Just then, Jess raised his head, ears back, eyes alert.

'What is it, Jess?' Jenny said, laying a hand on the dog's neck.'

Jess scrambled to his feet and barked, his tail wagging.

'Ooh!' Paul exclaimed as Jess's plumy tail brushed his cheek. 'That tickles, Jess.'

Jenny smiled. Jess seemed to have taken Paul's mind off his worries – at least for a little while.

Jess strained forward and Jenny looked out across the fields. Down below them, beyond the tarn, was a horse and rider.

Paul raised his binoculars to his eyes. 'It's Ian,' he cried.

'That must be Mercury he's riding,' Jenny explained. 'Ian exercises him for Matt while he's at college.' Matt was home for the weekend but Fraser Miles had needed him to help on the farm.

'What a wonderful horse,' Paul breathed, as they watched the gleaming black creature canter across the fields towards them.

Jenny smiled. 'Ian and Matt have done wonders with him,' she said.

Mercury had belonged to Sheena Miles. Fraser Miles had sold the horse immediately after the accident that had killed his wife. But Matt had found Mercury a few months later at the livestock market in Greybridge, a local town. The horse had been in a very sorry state.

He had been ill-treated and was extremely nervous.

At first Jenny had feared and hated Mercury, blaming the horse for her mother's death. But later, her father had explained that the accident had not been the horse's fault, and gradually Jenny had come to love Mercury.

Jess barked again and looked pleadingly at Jenny.

'All right,' Jenny said to him. 'Go on! Go and say hello to Mercury.'

Quick as the wind, Jess was off, streaking downhill towards the horse and rider.

'Jess and Mercury are great friends,' Jenny explained to Paul. 'When Mercury first came back to Windy Hill he was very nervous but Jess really helped to calm him down.'

Paul's eyes turned back to the Border collie as he scampered down the hill past fallen rocks, skirting the tarn and scaring ducks into the air.

'Wow! A diver!' Paul cried, training his binoculars on the flight of birds Jess had alarmed.

Jenny looked at Paul. He seemed much

happier now. Maybe he would forget his fears, she thought, as she raised her head to watch the birds wheeling against the sky. She frowned as she felt a large drop of rain on her upturned face. More followed, quickly spattering her cheeks and hair.

Well-prepared, she and Paul pulled on their hoods and zipped up their waterproof jackets. The clouds were huge now, low and threatening. As Jenny wiped the rain from her cheeks, a flash of lightning lit up the sky and she heard the first rumble of thunder. It sounded very near. Another flash followed and the thunder rolled even nearer. The heavens opened and the rain began to fall more heavily.

Jenny was about to beckon Paul up to shelter in the keep, when he grabbed her arm.

'Look!' he cried.

She turned at the alarm in the little boy's voice. 'What is it?' she asked, anxiously. Then she saw where he was pointing. As yet another streak of lightning flashed across the sky, Mercury reared up on his two hind legs in terror. Thunder rolled, seeming to rebound off the walls of the keep. Jenny's heart thundered

too for this had happened once before.

Mercury's forelegs came crashing down again and he began to gallop furiously. Jenny could see Ian hanging on grimly, straining at the reins, trying to hold the big horse. She caught her breath in horror as she watched Mercury race, out of control, across the turf below them. It seemed that Mercury, too, was remembering that terrible storm of the previous year.

'He's bolted!' Paul cried. 'Mercury is running away!'

Jenny grabbed the binoculars and focused them on Ian, trying desperately to see through the pouring rain. Ian's face was set and white; his hands gripped the reins.

The lightning flashed and flashed again. Jenny could feel the force of the thunder when it came. Mercury tossed his head and reared again in blind panic.

Then Jenny was running down the hill. Behind her, Paul called out in alarm.

'We've got to stop them,' Jenny called back, for once forgetting to face Paul as she spoke to him. 'The storm has frightened Mercury. He's running blind. Ian is going to be killed if we can't do something!'

Jenny ran on, her heart thumping, the breath ragged in her throat, the rain washing over her. Down the hill she pounded, leaping over fallen rocks, heedless of rabbit-holes that might trip her up. At the bottom she plunged forward, racing round the tarn, praying she could do something, *anything*, to stop Mercury before Ian was pitched off his back. For this was how Jenny's mother had been killed.

3

The breath rasped in Jenny's throat as she raced towards the horse and rider. Jess was already scrabbling over the rough drystone wall below the keep. Jenny saw Ian try again to rein in the big horse, twisting his body, gripping desperately with his legs to find control over the animal. Mercury reared and Jenny's breath stopped altogether as she saw Ian clinging to the reins and saddle. Then Jess reached the top of the wall and leaped for the ground beyond.

'No, Jess!' Jenny cried. But the little dog was over and running for the horse. Jenny reached the wall herself and clung to the rough stones, panting, as Paul came up behind her.

The little boy threw himself at the wall, heaving himself up on to it.

Jenny reached out an arm and grabbed him, turning him towards her. 'If you go running over there you'll frighten Mercury even more,' she said, breathlessly. 'That isn't the way to save Jess — or Ian.'

Paul looked at her. 'But what are we going to do?' he asked.

Jenny shook the rain from her eyes. 'I'm going to go over — very quietly. Stay here, Paul — please.'

Paul nodded again. 'Be careful,' he whispered.

Jenny laid a hand on the wall and pulled herself up, slipping on the wet stones. Jess had almost reached Mercury now. She kept her eyes on him as she dropped carefully over the wall and began to walk towards the terrified horse.

Ian had somehow managed to bring Mercury out of his headlong gallop but the horse's eyes were rolling and he reared again as another streak of lightning split the sky.

Ian turned and caught sight of her. Then all his attention was on the reins again as he brought Mercury down, leaning well into the saddle. Jenny could see his lips moving. He was talking to the horse, trying to calm him.

Jenny saw Jess stop within a metre of Mercury. The young dog laid back his ears and crouched low to the ground, crawling forward until he was almost under Mercury's dancing hoofs. Jenny forced herself not to call out but she couldn't help increasing her pace a little.

Then she stopped in her tracks as she realised what Jess was doing. The Border collie was working true to his instinct. Moving slowly, close to the ground, he made his way towards Mercury.

Mercury whinnied and for a moment his hoofs stopped dancing, then he threw his head up and neighed. Jess barked once, then crawled forward, lying right in front of the horse's forefeet. Jenny held her breath. If Mercury reared now he would come down on top of the collie. Jess wouldn't stand a chance.

She glanced quickly at Ian. His hair was

plastered to his head with the rain but his green eyes were intent. focused on Jess. He leaned forward, daring to take one hand off the reins, and laid a hand on Mercury's neck.

The big horse bent his head towards the little dog and Jess reached up, nuzzling Mercury's nose. Jenny watched, hardly breathing, as the two animals seemed to communicate with each other. Then Mercury took a step back and gradually his body seemed to relax.

Lightning tore through the sky again, but more distant now. Mercury flinched, but didn't rear up. Thunder rolled, but Mercury remained calm. Then the rain eased, and stopped as suddenly as it had begun.

Jenny looked at Ian and saw him relax too. He slid gently from Mercury's back on to the ground and staggered a little.

Jenny went to him as he leaned against Mercury's flank, resting his hand on the horse's neck. Mercury blew gently through his lips and shook his head slowly from side to side.

'Are you all right?' Jenny asked Ian anxiously.

Ian nodded. He was still pale and shaken. 'My legs feel like jelly,' he confessed. 'Can you hold

Mercury's head while I sit down for a minute?'

Jenny took the reins and stroked Mercury's neck, murmuring to him, but the horse was calm now – thanks to Jess.

Ian flopped down on the wet grass and lay there, looking up at her. 'Phew!' he said. 'What happened?'

Jenny didn't answer his question. She frowned. 'Have you ridden Mercury up here before?' she asked.

Ian nodded. 'Any number of times,' he replied. 'He's never bolted before. I can't understand it.'

'It must have been the storm,' Jenny explained. She bit her lip, her eyes shadowed. 'Do you remember Dad explaining how my mother got killed here last summer?' she asked Ian. 'Mum was riding Mercury towards the keep to take shelter from a sudden storm. They were just about to jump the wall below the keep when a bolt of lightning brought a tree down right in front of them. Mercury must have been terrified when the storm blew up today. I was scared it was all going to happen again.'

Ian's mouth dropped open. 'Oh, Jenny, you must feel awful,' he said. 'I'm sorry I gave you such a fright but I just couldn't control him.'

'It wasn't your fault,' Jenny assured him. 'But I think we should get Mercury home and talk to Dad and Matt about this.'

Ian looked at her seriously. 'You always said Mercury was dangerous,' he said.

Jenny nodded. 'I know,' she confessed. 'I blamed him for killing Mum. But it wasn't his fault. Not last time and not this time either. It must have been awful for him when the lightning began.'

'But if he's going to bolt every time there's a storm then he *is* dangerous,' Ian said, his face troubled.

'Jess managed to calm him,' Jenny replied thoughtfully. 'Maybe he just needs time to forget how frightened he was last time.'

'What's your dad going to say?' Ian asked, shoving his hair out of his eyes. 'Do you think he'll give Mercury more time? Or do you think he'll get rid of him?'

Jenny looked at Jess and Mercury. 'I don't know,' she replied. 'But Jess would miss Mercury so much – and so would Matt. And I'd miss him too, now.'

There had been a time, only weeks ago, when Jenny would gladly have got rid of Mercury. Now she felt quite differently about the big horse. She had seen for herself how gentle and affectionate he could be when she had ridden him in the Graston Parade at the end of the lambing season.

'Can I come over now?' called a small voice.

Jenny turned. 'Oh, Paul,' she answered apologetically. 'I'm sorry. Of course you can. Everything is all right now.'

Paul scrambled over the wall and came to stand beside them. 'Jess was really brave, wasn't he?' he said, bending down and giving Jess a pat.

Jenny nodded. Then a thought struck her. 'So were you, Paul,' she said.

The little boy looked up, surprised. 'Me?' he said.

'Yes, you!' replied Jenny. 'You were all set to climb over the wall to save Jess. I'll tell you something, Paul: whatever anybody says, you're a very brave boy.'

Paul looked up at her, his face breaking into a smile. 'Brave,' he repeated. 'Just like Jess.'

4

Jenny and Ian found Mr Miles in the farmyard, unloading supplies of insecticide from the jeep for the sheep dipping. The sheep Nell and Jake had gathered were already waiting in the holding pen before being dipped in the swimbath.

Fraser Miles turned to wave to them. 'I was getting a little worried about you, being out in that storm—' He stopped as he saw the expressions on their faces. 'What's happened?' he asked, as Jenny and Ian led Mercury into the farmyard.

Jess scampered over to Jake and Nell, wagging his tail. The two dogs lay still, allowing the puppy to nuzzle them.

'Mercury bolted,' Ian explained, unsaddling the horse. 'I was riding him up towards Darktarn Keep as the storm blew up, and he panicked.'

'Are you hurt?' Fraser asked urgently.

Jess looked up and barked at the sharp tone of Mr Miles's voice. Jenny laid a hand on his neck. 'It's all right, Jess,' she whispered.

'We're OK, Mr Miles,' Ian said quickly.

Jenny looked at her father. Fraser Miles's blue eyes looked worried.

'Nobody got hurt, Dad,' she reassured him. 'Little Paul McLay was up there too but we sent him home. We didn't think it would be a good idea to bring him back to Windy Hill.'

'His father certainly wouldn't like that,' Fraser agreed. 'Now, tell me exactly what happened.'

Jenny took a deep breath and began to explain. 'It was the storm that scared Mercury, I'm sure of that,' she finished, as Ian rubbed the big horse down. 'And if it hadn't been for Jess I don't know if we'd have got him calmed down.'

Fraser smiled. 'Jess has always been able to calm Mercury,' he said. 'You often find that with nervous horses. Being around a smaller animal seems to reassure them. Sometimes it's a cat or even a goat.' Then Fraser Miles looked serious. 'But if Mercury is going to bolt like that then we'll have to think again about keeping him. I'm not prepared to keep a dangerous animal,' he told Jenny firmly. 'I'll talk to Matt about it.'

'But it was the storm,' Jenny protested weakly. 'It came so suddenly — Mercury was frightened.' But she knew her father was right. She had been terrified herself that Ian would be thrown, as her mother had been.

Her father's eyes darkened. 'And what if there's another sudden storm when Ian or Matt is out on Mercury? They might get thrown next time — and we know what can happen then, don't we?' He put a hand on Jenny's shoulder. 'Look lass, we know Mercury didn't mean to harm your mother. And he didn't mean any harm to Ian today. But this panicking in storms – you must see I can't run any more risks like that.'

Jenny looked at her father in dismay. Poor Matt. He would be devastated. And poor Mercury.

'But if he really *is* dangerous, you couldn't sell him, could you?' asked Ian.

Jenny's heart lurched. She hadn't thought of that. If they couldn't sell Mercury, then he might have to be put down! She couldn't bear to think about it.

'Someone might be willing to take him and try to school the fear out of him,' Fraser replied. 'If not, then we'll have to send him to an animal sanctuary on the understanding that nobody can ride him.'

Jenny breathed a sigh of relief. At least the very worst wasn't going to happen.

Mr Miles whistled to his two dogs. Nell and Jake came to heel at once and followed Fraser out of the farm gate.

'I've got to get these sheep dipped,' Mr Miles said as he closed the gate. 'Don't take Mercury out again unless you have my permission, Ian. Matt's inside. Tell him he isn't to take him out

either. I've got to think this through.'

Jenny and Ian looked at each other in dismay.

'Oh dear! What's Matt going to say?' Jenny asked. 'He loves Mercury.'

'We'd better go and tell him,' Ian said glumly. 'It's all my fault. If I'd been a better rider this would never have happened.'

'No, Ian,' Jenny replied. 'It was the storm, not your riding that caused Mercury to panic. You did well to stay on him while he was bolting.' She sighed. 'I'm afraid Dad is right. Mercury's fear of storms does make him dangerous to have around.'

'Come on,' Ian said. 'Let's get Mercury stabled and find Matt.'

Matt was in the kitchen with Ellen Grace. There was a delicious smell coming from the oven as Mrs Grace bent to take out a baking tray.

'That smells great!' said Matt.

'Ah, I might have known you two would appear just as these were ready,' Mrs Grace said, smiling, as she saw Jenny and Ian. Then her face changed. 'You look as if you've lost a pound and found a penny. What's wrong?'

Jenny and Ian told their story again.

Matt listened intently, his blue eyes concerned. 'I've never had Mercury out in a storm. It must have reminded him so much of what happened last time. Horses can be amazing sometimes, the way they remember things.'

'The place wouldn't seem the same without Mercury, now,' Mrs Grace said sympathetically, as she placed a pot of tea and a plate of hot scones on the kitchen table.

'A lot of things look like changing, Ellen,' Matt replied, taking a scone. 'What are we going to do if *you* leave us?'

Jenny drew in her breath. In her concern about Mercury, she had forgotten her worry about Mrs Grace. The lease on the cottage she rented was nearly at an end, and her landlord, Calum McLay, had refused to renew it. It seemed this was because Ellen Grace now worked for Fraser Miles, whom Calum disliked. 'How long have you got now, Mrs Grace?' she asked.

'There's another month before my lease runs out,' the housekeeper told her, sighing. 'I've been looking around but there isn't another cottage to let in the area. It looks as if I'm going to have to move quite far away.'

Ian's mouth set stubbornly. 'There must be something we can do about Calum McLay,' he said. 'He's nothing but a troublemaker. He shouldn't be able to force you out of your home.'

'He *can* force me out because he owns the cottage,' Ellen Grace said quietly. 'There isn't a thing we can do.'

Jenny opened her mouth to make a suggestion. She'd had an idea growing in her mind for some time now. Why couldn't Mrs Grace move into Windy Hill? There was plenty of room for her and Ian. But Jenny knew she needed to speak to her father about it first. She would ask him just as soon as she could.

'I reckon Fiona takes after her dad rather than her mum,' she said instead. 'She's being really rotten to Paul. She's scaring him stiff with horror stories about going into hospital.'

'That's awful,' Ellen Grace said. 'Can't you speak to her – tell her to stop?'

Jenny shrugged. 'I can try,' she said. 'But Fiona never listens to anybody – especially me.'

'If she's anything like her father there's no point in *anyone* talking to her,' Matt said, getting up from the table. 'I'm just going to have a look at Mercury, then I've got to get back to college. I've got loads of reading to do for Monday and if I stay here, I know I won't get it done,' he said, smiling.

Jenny watched him go. He didn't look like his usual self at all. His feet dragged as he made his way to the door. 'Dad says he wants to talk to you before he does anything about Mercury,' she offered as he opened the door.

Matt turned and smiled slightly. 'At least that means Mercury will still be here when I come home next weekend,' he said. 'That's something, I suppose.'

Jenny sighed. Matt had put so much work into restoring Mercury to health. He must feel it was all for nothing.

She looked around the table. Ian was staring into his cup, the scone on his plate untouched. Mrs Grace was looking out of the window. She looked so sad. Jenny thought of Paul and his worries about going into hospital. She sighed again. Mercury, Mrs Grace's lease – and Paul.

Right now the world seemed full of problems.

She sat up. She could almost *hear* Carrie's voice saying, '*That's no way to think!* Do *something!*'

Well, she *would* do something. She would speak to her father about Mrs Grace coming to live at Windy Hill and she would try and talk to Fiona. But what about Mercury? There didn't seem any hope of a solution to *that* problem.

5

Jenny tried to speak to Fiona about Paul at school on Monday but Fiona wasn't in the mood to listen – not that she ever *was* in the mood to listen to Jenny.

'Why don't you mind your own business?' Fiona sneered.

'But Paul is only seven,' protested Jenny. 'You're scaring him with all your stories.' She shoved her hair out of her eyes. Jenny's hair always reflected her moods. Right now it was nearly standing on end, she was so angry.

'Little Miss Busybody,' Fiona said nastily. 'And just look at your hair. Haven't you ever *heard* of a hairbrush?' Fiona flicked her sleek short hair into place and flounced off, leaving Jenny fuming. Fiona was always making rude comments about Jenny's appearance – saying she couldn't afford new trainers or decent clothes.

'Don't take any notice of her,' Carrie advised, coming to stand beside Jenny.

'I don't care what she says about me,' Jenny replied. 'But why is she being so cruel to Paul? He's her brother. It's just so frustrating!'

'If you ask me, I reckon she's jealous of Paul,' Carrie replied thoughtfully.

Jenny looked at her friend in astonishment. Carrie's usually cheerful face was serious for once. 'But why?' she asked.

'Maybe Fiona thinks Paul gets too much attention at home,' Carrie went on. 'I heard her telling him he was a mummy's boy just the other day.'

'But that's ridiculous,' Jenny retorted. 'He's only little and he isn't spoiled. How can she be jealous of him? He's the one that's deaf. I just don't understand her.'

Carrie shook her head. 'Of course you don't understand her,' she agreed. 'I can't imagine you being jealous of anybody. But you've got to look at it from Fiona's point of view. Maybe she feels left out at home. Perhaps it seems that Paul is getting all the attention because of his deafness.'

Jenny opened her mouth to protest but closed it again. Maybe Carrie had a point. 'You might be right, Carrie,' she admitted. 'But I don't think I'll ever understand Fiona.'

'Well, thank goodness for that,' Carrie replied, grinning. 'I reckon you're far to nice to understand a creep like Fiona.'

Jenny couldn't help smiling. But a doubt nagged at the back of her mind. If what Carrie said was true then maybe Fiona wasn't such a creep after all; maybe she was just insecure. But that still didn't justify what she was doing to Paul.

'I'd like to ask Paul over to Windy Hill to play with Jess,' she confided to Carrie. 'He really likes Jess and it cheers him up such a lot, but his father would never let him visit us.'

Carrie looked thoughtful. 'It doesn't have to be Windy Hill,' she said at last. 'I could ask Paul to Cliff House – after all, you often come to see me, and you know how much Jess likes his runs on Cliffbay beach. If Paul just happened to be there at the same time . . .'

'Carrie, you're brilliant!' Jenny exclaimed.

'Oh, I know *that*,' Carrie agreed. 'But how about talented, beautiful, charming – let's see, what else?'

Jenny grinned. 'Anything you like,' she said. 'Let's go and find Paul.'

On Friday afternoon, Mrs Turner pulled up outside school in her orange Mini to pick up Carrie, Jenny and Paul. She had Jess with her. She'd collected him from Windy Hill on her way. Jenny grinned as she saw her pet's black-and-white face gazing out of the car window. The young collie gave them a joyful welcome as they climbed into the car.

'Ow!' Jenny protested as Jess hurled himself at her. 'You're getting heavy, Jess.' But Jess took no notice, licking her face ecstatically.

'I think he's gorgeous!' Paul announced, and Jess promptly launched himself at the little boy.

By the time they got to Cliffbay, Jess had calmed down and was lying comfortably across Jenny's lap, his head on Paul's knees. Jenny glanced at Paul and smiled. The little boy was stroking Jess's ears contentedly. What a pity he didn't have a pet of his own.

'Mum says she'll send Fiona to collect me later,' Paul said as Mrs Turner pulled up in front of Cliff House.

'I rang your mum,' Mrs Turner told him. 'She said that Fiona will come in time to take you home for tea – but that doesn't mean you can't have a quick snack. How would you like that?'

'I'd love it,' Paul said, as Jess scrambled out of the car, his tail wagging. 'And I'm going to love playing with Jess too.'

Jenny looked out to sea as they made their way down to the beach from Cliff House after tucking into apple juice and raisin biscuits. It was calm now but Jenny knew how quickly that could change. The storm at the keep had been the first of several. Luckily Mr Miles had managed to get the flock dipped between storms. Now his major worry was the effect of the weather on the lambs. They were still only a couple of months old and very dependent on their mothers for food and warmth. Mr Miles had had to take quite a few of the ewes and their lambs into the shearing shed for protection during the bad spell.

Jenny had enjoyed having the little black-faced lambs around the farm, but she knew they were better off out on the hills where they could learn to graze by watching their mothers. They would be weaned in another two months' time and they needed to learn to survive on their own.

'Dad put the lambs back out in the fields this morning now that the weather has improved,' she said to Carrie, as they watched Paul throwing a stick for Jess.

Carrie plonked herself down on the sand and looked up at her friend. 'Thank goodness those storms are over,' she said. 'My dad hasn't been able to take the boat out all week, it's been so bad. A lot of the fishing boats have been tied up at Cliffbay too.'

Jenny looked up at the sky. It was swept clean by rain and wind and the sun was shining. She sat down beside Carrie, enjoying the sunshine.

'Fetch, Jess!' Paul yelled, throwing the stick into the sea.

Jess bounded off, plunging into the water, swimming strongly. In no time at all he was back, ready to fetch again. Paul bent and fussed over him then he threw the stick once more.

'He'll never let you stop, Paul,' Jenny called when the little boy turned to grin at them.

Paul's grin widened. 'I could do this all day,' he replied. 'I'd never get tired of it.'

Jess ran up the beach, the stick in his mouth, and shook himself all over Paul but the little boy only laughed and made even more fuss of the young collie.

Jenny and Carrie lolled on the shore, watching Paul and Jess scamper around. Jenny was happy just to watch. Paul and Jess were having a marvellous time and, as she told Carrie, she could play with Jess any time she wanted. For Paul, this was really special.

Paul was soon wet through but the sun would dry him off. Jess came racing up the beach, stopped and shook himself, spraying Paul all over again.

'Good boy,' Paul said, bending down to pat the collie. Jess's tail wagged harder than ever as Paul held the stick up.

Jenny waved to catch the little boy's attention. 'Throw it further out, Paul,' she said, miming the action. 'Jess likes to swim.'

Paul nodded and threw the stick as far as he could.

Carrie screwed her eyes up against the sun, watching Paul and Jess.

'Those two get on really well,' she said.

Jenny nodded. 'Jess is wonderful with Paul,' she replied. 'It's amazing to watch. He never barks to get Paul's attention. He always puts himself where Paul can see him. It's as if he knows that Paul can't hear him.'

Carrie watched as Jess came scampering back up the beach. Paul had turned away to look at a fishing boat just setting out from the harbour at Cliffbay but, instead of barking, Jess ran across the beach until he was in Paul's direct line of vision.

'I see what you mean,' Carrie said admiringly.

'That's clever of Jess.'

'They're working out a kind of communication between them,' Jenny told her. 'It's quite different from the way Jess behaves with me.'

'Wow!' said Carrie. 'It's impressive.'

'I was wondering if it would be good for Paul to have a pet of his own,' Jenny said thoughtfully.

Carrie considered for a moment. 'I think that's a great idea,' she agreed. 'Do you think he would be allowed to have a puppy?'

Jenny shrugged. 'I don't know,' she replied. 'I don't want to suggest it to him in case he ends up disappointed. I wondered about mentioning it to Fiona, but she wouldn't listen to me.'

'Can you imagine suggesting *anything* to Fiona? Or Mr McLay, for that matter?' Carrie asked gloomily. 'They're both impossible.'

'That's what I thought,' Jenny replied. 'But what about *Mrs* McLay? I've only met her a couple of times but she seems really nice.'

'Yes, my mum seems to like her, too,' Carrie agreed. 'Have you got a puppy in mind?'

Jenny shook her head. 'I thought I would ask Mr Palmer,' she replied. 'If there just happened to be a puppy looking for a home, maybe Mrs McLay would agree.' Tom Palmer was the vet in Graston. He had treated Jess's bad leg and, since then, Jenny and the vet had become good friends.

Carrie smiled at Jenny. 'Good idea, Jen. It can't do any harm – so long as you don't get Paul's hopes up before we know whether or not he'd be allowed a puppy.'

'Maybe if he had a puppy to look forward to he'd be happier about going into hospital,' Jenny mused. 'He'd be a marvellous pet owner.'

There was a sound behind them and Jenny looked up. Fiona McLay stood over her, blocking the sun. Jenny scrambled to a half-sitting position. 'Hi, Fiona,' she said pleasantly.

'I've come to collect Paul,' the other girl said shortly. 'Were you talking about him just now?'

'You mean about the puppy?' Jenny said. 'It was just an idea. He and Jess get on so well together.'

'I've told you before, Jenny Miles,' Fiona snapped. 'Mind your own business. Paul can't have a puppy. He can't even hear.'

'What difference does that make?' Carrie

protested. 'Deaf people have hearing dogs. The dogs help them – just like guide dogs for the blind.'

'Keep out of it, Carrie,' Fiona retorted. She turned once again to Jenny. 'If Dad knew Paul was down here with you he'd be furious,' she said. 'He wouldn't want any of your daft ideas about dogs either.'

'A puppy,' said a small voice. 'For me?'

Jenny looked round, horrified. Paul had come up behind her. He had obviously read his sister's lips. 'It was only an idea, Paul,' she said.

Paul's eyes were shining. 'I'd *love* a puppy like Jess,' he said.

'Well you can't have one,' Fiona snapped. 'Mum's got enough to do looking after you without a puppy as well.'

Paul's face fell and Jenny's heart went out to him as she saw his disappointment.

Fiona didn't seem to notice. She put her hands on her hips and looked sternly down at Paul. 'It's time to go home,' she said. 'If Dad hears you've been playing with Jenny Miles you'll be in trouble.'

'It isn't Paul's fault,' Jenny protested, scrambling to her feet. 'It was my idea.'

Fiona turned to her. 'You've got too many ideas, Jenny Miles,' she sneered. 'Just keep them to yourself in future. Don't you *dare* mention anything about a puppy to my parents.'

With that, she grabbed Paul's hand and marched him up the beach towards the cliff path.

Jenny watched them go, fuming. Paul turned back once and gave them a wave, then they were lost to sight round the headland. 'What is *wrong* with her?' she said.

'Do you have to ask?' Carrie replied.

Jenny sighed. 'I suppose she'd be even more jealous of Paul if he got a puppy,' she said. 'Maybe I'd better give up the idea. The last thing I want to do is make Fiona resent Paul even more.'

Carrie shook her head. 'Just look at Jess,' she said. The Border collie was standing with the stick in his mouth, looking hopefully after Paul. 'It's a pity Paul might not be able to have a dog of his own — just because we don't want to upset horrible Fiona.'

Jenny threw herself down on the sand and looked up at the sky. It was blue from hills to horizon – not a cloud to be seen. She wished life was like that. Just at the moment she seemed to have quite a few problems.

'There is *one* thing I can do,' she said, sitting up determinedly.

'What's that?' asked Carrie.

'I can talk to Dad about Mrs Grace coming to live with us,' Jenny said firmly. 'At least I can solve *one* problem – maybe!'

6

'Come on,' said Carrie. 'Time for tea. You're coming to us, remember?'

Jenny rose and walked slowly along the beach with Carrie, calling to Jess. The puppy scampered up, wagging his tail and licking Jenny's hand. Jenny kneeled down and gave him a cuddle. 'Did you hear what Paul said, Jess?' she asked. 'He said he'd *love* a puppy like you.'

Jess's tail wagged even harder and he sat down

abruptly on the sand. Jenny laughed and felt better. Jess could always make her feel better.

Carrie's parents made her feel better too. They were both in the kitchen when the girls arrived. Mr Turner was ladling spaghetti into a big white bowl. Mrs Turner gave the bolognese sauce a final stir and tipped it over the pasta. She had obviously spent the day painting. There was a smear of bright blue paint on her cheek.

She rubbed at it absently when Carrie pointed it out. 'I've just had Tom Palmer on the phone,' she announced. 'He's got an abandoned puppy he wants to find a home for and he wants me to put a notice on the harbour notice-board.' She chuckled. 'He suggested I do a little illustration. It's a Border terrier. I think a little sketch would look sweet.'

'What!' screeched Carrie. 'But we were just talking about asking Mr Palmer to find a puppy for little Paul McLay. This is amazing! It's like we made it happen!'

'Does Paul want a puppy?' Mr Turner asked Jenny, as he sat down at the kitchen table.

'*He* would love one,' said Jenny. 'But we haven't actually mentioned it to his parents.'

'I see,' said Mr Turner, his blue eyes twinkling. 'Do I smell a plot?'

'Just a tiny one,' Carrie grinned. 'But don't you see? This is a *sign*! Paul wants a puppy. We were talking about getting him a puppy! And now Mr Palmer has a puppy that needs a home! It's fate!'

'Mmm,' said Mrs Turner, setting plates out in front of them all. 'I don't know about fate but it would certainly be convenient.'

'Fate,' repeated Carrie firmly. 'This puppy was *sent* for Paul. Just you wait and see.'

Mr Turner looked at Jenny and winked. 'Oh well,' he said. 'In that case there's no problem.' Then he turned to his wife. 'Don't bother about the notice, Pam. That puppy is home and dry!'

Home and dry, Jenny thought as she reached the top of the cliff path on her way home after tea. She turned and looked out to sea. Puffin Island was still bathed in sunlight but now Jenny could see a mass of clouds beginning to gather on the horizon. She shivered. Maybe there were more storms to come after all.

'Come on, Jess,' she called to her pet. 'Time to go home!'

As Jenny and Jess raced into the farmyard, Jenny let out a whoop of delight. 'Matt's home!' she cried delightedly. 'There's his motorbike, Jess!' For a moment her pleasure was tinged with concern as she remembered that this weekend her father would decide Mercury's fate. He had been waiting until Matt returned.

Jess barked madly and wagged his tail, streaking towards the kitchen door. Jenny followed at a run.

'Where's Matt, Mrs Grace?' Jenny called, as she and Jess burst into the kitchen. Ian was sitting at the kitchen table, his homework spread out before him.

Mrs Grace smiled. 'And hello to you too,' she said.

Jenny looked apologetic. 'Oops, sorry. Hello, Mrs Grace. Hi, Ian! – where's Matt? Has Dad said anything about Mercury?'

Mrs Grace laughed. 'One question at a time. Matt is out helping your father to move all the sheep into the top field. They're driving the flock up the track now. Your dad reckons there's

64

another storm on the way and the bottom field is already waterlogged. I don't think they've had time to talk about Mercury yet.'

'Maybe I should go and help them,' Jenny suggested, a frown creasing her brow. Her father had so much work to do looking after the sheep all on his own. Matt had managed to be at Windy Hill for the lambing, but for the rest of the college term he was only able to be home to help at weekends.

'He'd be better pleased if you got on with your homework – like Ian,' Mrs Grace replied, smiling.

'I offered to help,' Ian said, looking disappointed.

'I think your father and Matt can manage, Jenny,' Mrs Grace said firmly. 'They've probably finished by now, anyway.'

Jenny made a face. 'Lucky Matt. Helping on the farm is much more interesting than home-work,' she said. 'Isn't it, Jess?'

Jess gave a short bark and wagged his tail. He obviously agreed with Jenny.

At that moment the phone rang and Mrs Grace answered it. Jenny watched the housekeeper's face change from friendly interest to concern.

'When did this happen?' she asked sharply.

At once Jenny was all attention. Something was wrong.

Mrs Grace listened for a few moments more then spoke again. 'I'll let them know straight away,' she said. 'They'll come over to you immediately. I'm sure of that.'

'What is it, Aunt Ellen?' Ian asked as Ellen Grace put the phone down.

The housekeeper's face looked very serious. 'That was Anna McLay from Dunraven,' she answered. 'Paul's mother. She's in a dreadful state. Paul's gone missing.'

'Missing?' repeated Jenny. 'But I saw him this afternoon just before tea.'

Ellen Grace looked intently at her. 'Where?' she asked sharply.

'Down on the beach,' Jenny answered. 'He came with Carrie and me to Cliffbay, after school.'

'Did you leave him there on his own?' Mrs Grace asked.

Jenny felt herself flushing. 'No, of course not,'

she replied. 'Fiona came to take him home. They both went off together. The last time I saw them they were heading for the cliff path.'

Mrs Grace nodded. 'That fits,' she said. 'Anna McLay says Paul ran away from Fiona when she was bringing him home. He's been missing for two hours now.'

Jenny frowned. 'That's not like Paul,' she said. Then she flushed. 'He was a bit upset.'

Mrs Grace fired questions at her and Jenny answered as best she could, telling the house-keeper about her idea for a puppy for Paul.

'But Fiona said he couldn't have a puppy, it would be too much trouble,' Jenny finished. 'Do you think that's what made him run away?'

Mrs Grace shook her head. 'Who knows?' she said. 'The important thing is to find him. Anna McLay is out of her mind with worry. If he's up on the cliffs he could be in danger, and if he's wandered into the hills it might be even worse. The tarns up there are deep and the river is swollen from all the recent storms. Anna wants a search party organised straight away.'

'Have they told the police?' Ian asked.

Ellen Grace nodded. 'The police say two

hours isn't very long but they sent a patrol car out. The trouble is, a patrol car can't get into the hills. If they don't find him soon they'll call up Greybridge for police dog handlers and send out a search party on foot. Run and tell your father and Matt, Jenny. Tell them they're needed urgently. We've got to go and help find Paul.'

Jenny leaped to her feet. 'Come on, Jess,' she called. 'Let's go!'

Jenny ran so hard her heart was hammering by the time she got to the track. Ahead of her the road was crammed with sheep, all trying to get through the field gate at the same time. Jake and Nell were weaving amongst them, rounding up the stragglers, driving the last of the sheep forward and into the field. Her father was following behind his dogs.

Jenny ran forward, waving her arms. 'Dad! You've got to come quickly. Matt too!'

Fraser Miles turned. The sheep bleated and began to jostle one another. Mr Miles strode towards Jenny and bent down, scooping Jess up. 'Now, Jenny. You know I don't want Jess out with the sheep. He's a house dog.'

'I'm sorry, Dad,' Jenny apologised, taking Jess

from him. 'But this is an emergency.'

Matt whistled to Nell and Jake and shep-
herded the last of the sheep through the gate,
shutting it behind them. He turned and walked
back towards Jenny and her father. 'What's the
matter, Jen?' he asked.

'It's Paul McLay,' Jenny blurted out, putting
Jess back down on the track. 'He's gone missing
and the McLays are organising a search party.
They need all the help they can get.'

'Where did they last see him?' Fraser Miles
asked.

'Fiona lost him somewhere between the cliff
path and Dunraven,' she said breathlessly, as her
father began to stride down the hill towards
the farmhouse. Nell and Jake came to heel at
once.

'How long has he been missing?' Matt put
in.

'About two hours,' Jenny replied. 'The police
have sent out a patrol car but Mrs McLay is
afraid Paul is lost in the hills.'

'If he is we could have a devil of a job finding
him,' Mr Miles said. 'I'll take the jeep up there.'

'I'll get Mercury saddled up,' Matt said. 'A

horse can go places even a jeep can't.'

Fraser Miles hesitated. Jenny knew what he was thinking. Mercury hadn't been ridden since he'd bolted with Ian. But this was an emergency! Paul's life could be in danger. 'It was only the storm that spooked Mercury,' she said. 'He's OK otherwise.'

'All right, Matt,' Mr Miles said after a moment. 'But be careful.'

'I will,' Matt promised, beginning to run.

Jenny watched him vault over the wall that bordered the track, taking the shortest route back to the farm. 'What about me?' she asked.

'You?' her father said.

'I want to help look for Paul,' Jenny pleaded. 'Jess can help too. Jess knows Paul's scent.'

'You're far too young,' Fraser Miles told her. 'The last thing we want is another youngster lost on the hills.'

Jenny put a hand on her father's arm. She didn't dare put her real fear into words. She couldn't help thinking that maybe it was her fault Paul had run away. If she hadn't half promised him a puppy he wouldn't have been so disappointed when Fiona said he couldn't have one. Was that why he had run off?

'Please, Dad,' she pleaded. 'How would you feel if I got lost? You'd want everybody to help, wouldn't you?'

Fraser Miles stopped for a moment and looked down at her. 'I reckon I would,' he said. 'OK, but when I tell you it's time to go home, you go home. Right?'

'Right,' said Jenny. 'I promise.'

Jenny and Ian saw Carrie as soon as they arrived at Dunraven. She came running towards them. 'Mum and I came straight here. Mrs McLay called to tell us what had happened,' she said, her expression worried. 'I've tried to think but I don't remember Paul saying anything that might give us a clue.'

'Neither do I,' Jenny sympathised. 'But at least we can help search for him.'

The crowd of searchers gathered in the farmyard and stood listening attentively to Sergeant Scott from Graston police station.

'We've covered most of the roads round about,' he explained. 'That isn't to say the little boy couldn't be hiding in a ditch. But we've done the best we could. I'm afraid we can't ask for a search and rescue helicopter just yet. Paul hasn't been missing long enough to merit a full-scale operation.'

'How long does he have to be missing before you people take it seriously?' snapped Calum McLay. The big man's face was white with strain and he looked belligerently at Sergeant Scott.

'I know how you must be feeling, Mr McLay,' Sergeant Scott replied. 'But we're doing the best we can. Children that age often run off for a few hours, then they turn up as right as rain, wondering what all the fuss was about. We've already requested a couple of police dogs. They should be here any time now.'

'But Paul isn't the type to run off,' Mrs McLay protested. Paul's mother was usually a picture of neatness but now her fair hair was ruffled and her waxed jacket was dragged on just anyhow.

'Let's just get on with it,' Calum McLay ordered.

Sergeant Scott sighed. At the best of times, Calum McLay wasn't the easiest person to deal with. When he was as worried as he was now he was just impossible.

The sergeant handed out Ordnance Survey maps. 'I want a note of which route everyone is taking,' he explained. 'That way we can cover the most ground and keep a check on which parts have been searched. Matt Miles is going to patrol the search parties on his horse. We haven't got a rough terrain vehicle for the hills around here so we'll search there on foot while we still have daylight on our side.'

'That won't be long,' Ian whispered to Jenny. 'Look at those clouds.'

Jenny hadn't noticed the weather. Ian was right. The clouds did look threatening. There was a frightening yellowish tinge to the under-side of them. She shivered. 'Let's just hope the weather holds for a while.'

'And let's hope Mr McLay's temper holds as well,' said Matt, behind them. 'He isn't doing anybody any good behaving like this.'

'Mrs McLay is really upset,' Ian commented.

Anna McLay was standing huddled in her jacket, wringing her hands. Jenny smiled ten-tatively at her.

Mrs McLay came across to them. 'I can't tell you all how grateful I am,' she said, her voice shaking with emotion. 'All these people turning out to look for Paul. It's so kind of you.'

'We all really like Paul a lot,' Ian said to her.

Mrs McLay smiled. 'I can see that,' she said. 'I didn't realise so many people knew him.'

'We'll find him, Mrs McLay,' Matt said.

Anna McLay nodded. 'I wish I could help in the search,' she said. 'The police think it would be better if I stayed here – just in case he comes back home.'

'I hope he does, Mrs McLay,' Carrie said. 'I hope he comes running in and you give him a good scolding for worrying everybody.'

A tear slid down Anna McLay's face. 'I'd be glad to,' she said. 'If only he *would* come running in the door I wouldn't mind what he'd done.'

Jenny watched sympathetically as Mrs McLay walked away. 'It must be so hard just having to wait,' she said.

Carrie nodded. 'At least when you're searching you feel as if you're doing something. Poor Mrs McLay. I like her a lot.'

'Fiona is upset too,' Jenny said. 'Look at her.

I'll go and have a word with her.'

Fiona McLay stood apart from the others. Her face was chalk white and streaked with tears. 'I know what you're going to say,' she burst out as Jenny came up to her. 'It's my fault, isn't it? That's what Dad thinks.'

'What happened exactly?' Jenny asked.

Fiona ran a hand through her short dark hair, making it stand on end. For once, she didn't seem to be bothered how she looked. 'Paul was in a bad mood all the way home,' she said distractedly. 'All he could talk about was that puppy. I told him he couldn't have one. How could he look after a puppy? He's deaf. And he's got to go into hospital. I certainly wasn't going to look after a puppy for him while he was in hospital, and Mum shouldn't have to either.'

'I shouldn't have said anything about a puppy,' Jenny said miserably.

'No, you shouldn't have,' Fiona retorted. Then she looked away and brushed a hand across her eyes. 'He ran away from me,' she went on. 'I thought he was just sulking. I thought if I walked on he would come to his senses and follow me.'

'But he didn't,' Jenny said.

Fiona shook her head. 'When I went back to look for him I was furious. Then I began to get scared. Where *is* he?' she wailed. She couldn't hold back a sob.

Jenny laid a sympathetic hand on Fiona's arm. 'We'll find him,' she said comfortingly.

Fiona swallowed. 'What if we don't?' she asked. 'What if he's out there, lying hurt? What if he's fallen into one of the tarns and drowned? What if he's fallen over the cliff and broken his leg? Or what – what if he's dead?' Fiona's voice was becoming hysterical.

Jenny took a deep breath, trying to keep her own voice calm. 'He's probably just lost,' she said. 'There are going to be loads of us searching, Fiona. We're bound to find him.'

Fiona turned on her. 'It's all right for you,' she said snappishly. 'You weren't the one who lost him. Nobody is blaming *you*!' She turned on her heel and walked away.

'Don't let her upset you,' Ian said, coming up behind Jenny.

Jenny sighed. 'Fiona's right though,' Jenny said. 'Nobody *does* blame me. But it might be my fault after all. If I hadn't mentioned a puppy maybe none of this would have happened.'

'So, there's only one thing to do,' said Ian.

'What's that?' Jenny asked.

Ian's green eyes were steady. 'Find him,' he said.

Dear Dad

7

Ian, Carrie and Jenny joined the search party led by Fraser Miles. They drove up into the hills as far as the jeep would take them, then Fraser handed out whistles.

'Remember, it's no good shouting,' he reminded them. 'Paul won't be able to hear you. We'll have to search every metre of ground. Spread out, and whatever you do, don't lose touch. If you come across any sign of Paul give three blasts on your whistle.'

Matt rode up on Mercury just in time to hear his father's last words. 'I'm going to be keeping all the search parties in contact,' he said. 'If you want to talk to me use the whistle. Mercury will hear it, even if I don't.'

'Why can't we use mobile phones?' Mrs Turner asked.

'We can – if they work,' said Fraser Miles. 'But up here in the hills the signals are pretty unreliable.'

Mrs Turner put her mobile back in her pocket. 'So much for modern technology,' she remarked. 'Let's get going.'

'Isn't your dad here?' Ian asked Carrie.

Carrie looked sideways at him. 'He's out in his boat,' she said.

Ian looked disapproving for a moment then his face changed. 'Oh, I see,' he said. 'Sorry I asked.'

'Why?' said Jenny, puzzled.

Carrie swallowed hard. 'Dad's doing a patrol of the sea beneath the cliffs with the other boats from Cliffbay,' she explained. 'It was high tide a couple of hours ago. The coastguard has sent a boat out too.'

Jenny felt herself go suddenly cold. 'Do the police think Paul might have fallen over the cliff?' she asked.

'They reckoned it was best to have a look,' Carrie said. 'They're searching between here and Puffin Island.'

Jenny looked out to sea. The water looked grey and cold beneath the cloudy sky and the waves were choppy.

'Come on, Jenny,' Ian urged her. 'We're ready to go.'

Jenny looked down at Jess. 'Find Paul,' she said urgently. 'The police dogs aren't here yet but you know his scent so well. Please, Jess, find Paul!'

Two hours passed. It was getting dark, and Jenny was footsore and weary. The police dogs had arrived more than an hour earlier, but there hadn't been any sign of the missing boy. It was hard work. They had to search every fold in the hill, every ditch, behind every rock. Paul could be lying unconscious, or hiding in fear, anywhere.

At last Fraser Miles called a break as Matt came riding up.

'No luck?' asked Matt.

Fraser shook his head.

'It's the same with the others,' Matt said. 'If we don't find him soon we're going to have an even harder job. The light is getting really bad now.' Matt was right. The dark storm clouds were quickly taking away the little that was left of the daylight. The rain couldn't hold off much longer.

'What's happening?' asked Mrs Turner. 'Are the police sending for reinforcements yet?'

Matt nodded. 'They're trying to get a helicopter now in order to search places we can't reach on foot, but it might take some time,' he said. 'The police dogs haven't been able to find any trace of Paul and the darker it gets the more difficult it is for the dog handlers. I'm going to take Mercury home and join up with the climbing party on the cliffs.'

Fraser Miles looked at Jenny's tired face. 'Take Jenny home too, will you, Matt?' he said. 'She looks dead-beat.'

Jenny looked up, appalled. 'But you can't send

me home, Dad,' she protested. 'We haven't found Paul yet.'

'Remember your promise,' Fraser said.

Jenny bent her head. She *had* promised to go home when her father told her to.

'I'm taking Carrie home too,' Mrs Turner said. 'What about you, Ian? Do you want a lift?'

'I'd better get in touch with Aunt Ellen,' Ian replied. 'Have you seen her, Matt?'

'She stayed at Dunraven to keep Paul's mum company,' Matt replied.

'I'll drop you off there as we pass,' Mrs Turner offered.

Ian nodded. 'I'll follow on to Windy Hill after I've seen Aunt Ellen,' he told Jenny. 'That way we can wait together for news.'

Matt reached out a hand to Jenny. 'Come on, Jen,' he said. 'Hop aboard. Mercury won't mind carrying the two of us home.'

Jenny put her foot in Matt's stirrup and he hauled her up, settling her in front of him. Mercury stood steady as a rock while she grasped his bridle. She turned and called Jess. The collie pup ran obediently over and fell into line beside the horse.

'Where are the police searching next?' Fraser called after his son as Matt turned Mercury's head.

'The far side of the bay and the hills above,' Matt called back. 'Somebody from Greybridge was driving to Cliffbay and saw someone up there an hour or so ago.'

'Was it Paul?' Jenny asked eagerly.

Matt shook his head. 'They don't think so,' he replied. 'The description didn't fit very well. The driver was a long way off. It could have been a hillwalker but it's the only lead they've got.'

They made their way back to Windy Hill, Jess running alongside. The hills beyond Cliffbay were the wildest in the area. Jenny hoped against hope that Paul wasn't lost up there. But then again, if he was, the police would be on his trail.

'Can you rub Mercury down for me?' Matt asked Jenny as he helped her down off the big horse's back. 'I want to get back up there as quickly as possible.'

Jenny nodded. 'Of course. Good luck, Matt!'

she said as her brother turned to go.

Matt smiled. 'We'll do the best we can,' he said. 'You know that.'

Jenny watched Matt set off. 'Oh, Jess,' she said, bending to give the young collie a hug. 'I hope they find him soon.'

Mercury whickered and Jenny looked up. 'It's OK, Mercury,' she said. 'I'm coming. Let's get you rubbed down.'

Jenny led Mercury into the stable and un-saddled him. She couldn't get her mind off Paul. Where *was* he? Wherever he was he must be feeling really bad. She wiped Mercury's flanks automatically, feeling the horse relax under her hands. She wished *she* could relax but she was too worried for that.

'If it wasn't so late I'd go up to Darktarn Keep, Jess,' she said.

Jenny's hands stopped moving and Mercury shifted uneasily, looking round at her. Jenny was remembering her conversation with Paul. She had told him the keep was where she always went when she got worried. He had liked the keep too. What if he had gone there? The searchers would never find him. They were looking in completely the wrong direction.

Jenny made a move towards the stable door. She should phone Mrs McLay. Then she stopped. She couldn't do that. What if she was wrong? She couldn't bear to think of getting Mrs McLay's hopes up all for nothing.

Jenny bit her lip. 'What am I going to do, Jess?' she asked.

Jess looked up at her, his head on one side.

In an instant Jenny made up her mind. She reached for Mercury's saddle. 'Sorry about this, boy,' she said to the horse. 'I know you were all ready to be tucked up in your stable but I've just got to check this out. If Paul is at the keep we've got to find him. It's dangerous up there – especially when it gets dark.'

Jenny threw the saddle over Mercury's broad back. 'You've got to help me, Mercury,' she whispered. 'You and Jess. If Paul is up there we have to find him. If he's hurt you'll have to carry him home, Mercury. Don't let me down, boy. Please don't let me down.'

Jenny gave Jess a drink, found a torch and scribbled a quick note for her father. She left the note on the kitchen table. Writing it took up precious time but the last thing she wanted was to have her father thinking she had gone missing too.

She led Mercury through the farm gate then climbed on to the fence. She had to stand on the fence to mount him.

'Steady, boy,' she murmured to him. 'I know you're tired but do this for me – and for Paul.'

She needed the big horse. Paul might be hurt. Parts of the keep were unstable. Jenny knew which areas to stay away from but Paul didn't. Anyway, Mercury could get to the keep far quicker than Jenny could on foot.

'Come on, Jess,' she called.

Jess pricked up his ears and trotted after Mercury, keeping close to the big horse's hoofs. Jenny smiled down at her pet. Jess was such a comfort.

As she rode up the track and out into the open ground above the top field she heard the rumble of thunder in the distance. She turned briefly and looked out to sea. The water was steel grey now, the waves rolling in topped by white caps which gleamed in the fading light. Above her, thick clouds held the promise of rain, and as she reached open country the first drops began to fall.

Jenny shivered as another roll of thunder sounded far in the distance. She only hoped it wasn't moving this way. If it did, would Mercury bolt again? Jenny pushed the thought away. She was halfway to the keep now. It would be as bad to turn back as to go on. She dug her heels into Mercury's flanks, urging him on.

'Come on, boy,' she whispered as another roll of thunder sounded in the distance. 'There's nothing to be afraid of.'

Jess ran along beside Mercury, keeping close to the big horse's hoofs. A sudden gust of wind whipped Jenny's hair over her face and she clawed it back. The rain was getting heavier now, stinging her face as it was blown on the wind.

Jenny peered into the gloom. Far above her was the keep. She could see its jagged outline, dark against the sky.

'That's where we're going, Mercury,' she whispered, bending low over the horse's ears. 'Darktarn Keep.'

Up ahead was the drystone wall and, beyond that, the tarn, glimmering in the failing light. At that moment Jenny heard a rumbling noise coming from the other side of the hill. The thunder *was* moving – and it was coming closer.

Mercury's head came up and he whinnied. Jenny clenched her hands on the reins then, very deliberately, relaxed them. She mustn't risk transmitting any of her nervousness to him.

'Jess!' she called softly.

Jess barked once and moved closer to the big horse, pacing him. Jenny felt Mercury's muscles bunch under her and Jess, seeming to sense his agitation, moved under the big horse. Immediately Mercury relaxed, his tense muscles softening.

'Good boy,' Jenny whispered, leaning close to his ear.

She rubbed her hand gently over his neck, murmuring to him, soothing him. Mercury's ears pricked and he turned his head a little, as if listening. Jenny went on talking in a low voice, hardly knowing what she was saying. After a moment she realised that it wasn't her words that were calming the big horse, it was the tone of her voice. As she felt him respond to her murmurs she grew in confidence, gripping less tightly with her knees, loosening the reins, showing Mercury that she had faith in him. And Mercury, his ears up, snuffled gently, his hoofs stepping firmly over the rough ground. Jenny sat up in the saddle, trying to see how far they were from the keep.

At that moment, another rumble of thunder sounded, much closer now. There was no doubt about it – a storm was building up. Jess wove his way in and out of Mercury's hoofs. 'We'll be all right, Jess,' Jenny called softly.

If only she could get to the shelter of the keep before the storm broke. Mercury whinnied nervously, and Jenny bent over his neck once more, whispering to him. To her relief, Mercury tensed, but did not shy at the next roll of thunder. His fear was under control – so far.

Jess barked and Jenny looked up. There was the keep, closer than she had thought.

'Come on, boy,' she murmured to Mercury. 'You can do it.'

Jenny steered Mercury away to the left to a break in the drystone wall, leaving the horse to pick his way through. Then they were passing the tarn, approaching the rise on which Darktarn Keep stood.

At the top of the rise, Jenny slid from the saddle and dropped to the ground. Her legs felt a little weak. A furry bundle launched itself at her and licked her hand. 'Oh, Jess, what would I do without you?' she said gratefully.

Then the thunder rolled louder. Jenny shivered, laying her hand on Mercury's neck. Mercury whickered and Jenny felt his warm breath on her cheek. She took hold of the reins, leading the horse towards the keep. 'There's no time to waste, Jess,' she said. 'Find Paul!'

Jess scampered over a low ruined wall and into the keep as Jenny led the big horse between the fallen stones of the wall of the building. Carefully, picking his way through the ruins, Mercury followed her until they came out into what had once been the courtyard of the keep.

Jess was standing in the middle of the court-yard, barking frantically. Jenny looked beyond

Jess, into the shadows of the far wall of the keep. Paul was sitting on the wall, his back to them. He hadn't noticed their approach.

Jenny's breath caught in her throat. The boy was sitting right on the edge of the wall, under the shelter of an overhanging archway. She knew exactly what was on the other side. That part of the wall dropped sheer into the river below. And Jenny knew the wall was unsafe.

Her first instinct was to run to Paul, and snatch him back from danger. But what if she startled him? What if he slipped and toppled over?

At that moment, before Jenny could do anything, a massive bolt of lightning flashed directly overhead.

Paul looked up, his terrified face illuminated for a moment in the searing light. He stood up, balancing precariously on the top of the narrow wall. As he turned he caught sight of Jenny.

She tried to smile reassuringly as she took a step towards him. She had to get him down from that wall. He didn't realise how dangerous it was.

Behind Jenny, Mercury shifted. Jenny turned

back to the big horse as the thunder followed the flash. She laid a hand on his flank. The last thing she wanted was Mercury to bolt now.

Mercury whickered and settled under her touch.

'Good boy,' Jenny muttered, relieved that the horse had stayed calm. She beckoned Jess over. 'Stay with Mercury, Jess,' she said to the puppy. Then she moved forward again towards Paul.

Another flash of lightning ripped through the sky immediately above. Jenny saw Paul's face turn upwards again and his look of shock was plain to see in the brief flash of the light. He moved as if to scramble down from the wall but his foot slipped and he teetered for a moment, rocking on his narrow perch.

'Paul!' Jenny cried, racing forward.

Overhead, the thunder rolled almost immediately, bouncing off the walls of the old ruined keep.

Jenny saw Paul's face, pale in the garish light, then he gave a cry as he shifted his position, trying to keep his balance. He stepped back, his left foot slipping on the wet surface of the stones. He spread his arms out to steady himself

but, as he did so, a shower of small stones fell from the archway above him, shaken loose by the force of the thunder. Paul put his hands up to protect himself as the stones rattled and bounced down on the wall beside him.

He took another step, his hands covering his head, but slipped again. He swayed on top of the wall, desperately trying to regain his balance.

Jenny rushed forward, but it was too late. Paul tipped backwards out of her reach, and fell from view.

8

'Oh, no! Paul!' Jenny cried. Lightning flashed and thunder rolled again. Jenny heard Mercury whinny behind her. She turned, alarmed at the sound, but Mercury was standing where she had left him, Jess at his heels, keeping him calm.

Jenny turned back to the wall, clinging to the stones. 'Paul!' she yelled into the darkness below.

The rain fell more heavily now, stinging her

eyes, washing down the wall under her hands in great sheets. She shook the hair out of her face and peered down. Below, she could hear the river roaring down the hill, surging and crashing against its banks.

It was no good. She couldn't see where the little boy had fallen. She clung to the wall, powerless to help. Then, as the next bolt of lightning lit up the area again, Jenny spotted him.

He had tumbled down to the bottom of the slope and into the river, but had managed to stop himself from being swept away by grabbing hold of a bush at the river's bank.

Her heart in her mouth, Jenny watched the little boy, half submerged in the roaring river, struggling to keep his head out of the foaming water as it rushed past him. She drew a hand across her eyes, clearing the rain from them. 'I'm coming, Paul!' Jenny yelled. 'Just hang on!'

The water tore at Paul's clothes. The bush was the only thing stopping him from being carried away by the river. How long would his grip hold?

'Jenny!' shouted a voice behind her.

Jenny turned, one foot already on the wall. 'Ian!' she cried. 'Thank goodness you're here!'

Ian was standing on the far side of the courtyard, his hand on Mercury's neck. He ran towards her. His hair was plastered close to his head as the rain beat down. 'I went back to Windy Hill and saw your note,' he gasped, taking a crumpled piece of paper from his pocket. 'I ran all the way. Did you ride Mercury in that storm?'

'He was all right,' Jenny said. 'He didn't bolt. He's safe. But, Ian, Paul isn't! He's in danger.'

'Is Paul *here*?' Ian asked.

Jenny looked at the dripping figure before her. 'You've got to help,' she urged. 'Paul was hiding in the keep. He's fallen into the river. Come on! We've got to save him.'

Then she was off, slipping and sliding down the wet grass. Jess, seeing Jenny race off, followed her.

'Be careful!' Ian yelled as he plunged after her.

Jenny could think of nothing else but getting to Paul in time. Then she called out in alarm as her foot slipped. She went down, her foot twisting under her painfully as she skidded several metres on her back, the river coming ever closer.

A second later Jess reached her and grabbed hold of her coat in his teeth, helping to slow her fall. Ian caught up with them and helped Jenny up. 'It won't do any good if we all end up in the river,' he said.

She nodded briefly and they edged their way cautiously down the rest of the slope until they reached level ground, Jess ahead of them. The roar of the water and the crash of thunder was so loud they could barely hear each other.

Jenny peered through the gloom. 'There!' she yelled, pointing.

Paul was floundering near the edge of the river, the water pouring around and over his terrified, white face, making him cough and splutter. Jenny could see now he was clinging to the root of a young tree that was sticking out of the riverbank. The recent storms had washed away the earth from the banking, exposing it.

'Quick, then,' said Ian. 'We should be able to reach him.'

But as he spoke, Jenny gasped in horror. 'Look! The tree root is coming away from the bank!'

With a tearing sound, the root Paul was clinging to broke free. Paul cried out in fright as the force of the water whirled him further out into the torrent. Luckily the root didn't break off entirely and Paul managed to hang on as the current dragged at it.

Jenny moved forward but Ian grabbed her. 'No,' he said. 'The river is flowing far too fast and he's too far out now. It's too dangerous.'

'But we have to do something!' Jenny cried, distraught. Paul's eyes were fixed on her. She couldn't think of leaving him even to get help. Then her face lit up. 'Mercury can help! Get Mercury, Ian. Hurry!'

Ian nodded and scrambled off up the slope.

'Ian!' Jenny called. 'You can ride him. It's quicker – but take Jess with you.'

Ian nodded again and beckoned Jess to him.

'Go on, Jess,' Jenny said. 'Go with Ian to Mercury. He might need you.'

The puppy bounded up the hill after Ian.

'I'll be as quick as I can!' Ian promised.

The wind was stronger than ever and lightning split the sky at intervals, followed by the crash of thunder. Jenny hoped that Mercury would stay calm. Ian would have to ride the horse down the far side of the hill and round the base of it.

She kept her eyes on Paul, willing the little boy to hang on, hoping against hope that his fingers would not slip on the wet tree root.

It seemed like years before Ian was back, riding Mercury towards the river, with Jess at the big horse's side.

Jenny made a grab for Mercury's bridle. 'If we can get the reins out to Paul we can pull him in,' she said.

Ian nodded, helping her with the buckles. The leather straps were slippery with rain but at last they managed to get the reins loosened and coupled together again into a long strap.

Jenny took hold of the length of leather and tried to cast it out into the water. Paul's hand came up as he saw what they were doing but the wind beat back upon them, defying their efforts. The reins were not heavy enough to withstand the wind.

'Don't let go, Paul,' Jenny mouthed. 'Don't let go of the tree root.'

'We'll never do it,' said Ian, defeated. His face was running with water, his hair tangled and wet. 'Can't we find something heavy to attach to the reins?'

Jenny shook her head. 'What if we hit Paul? We can't risk throwing anything heavy.'

Jenny scraped a soaking strand of hair away from her own face. She felt frustration rise in her as Jess stood on the riverbank, barking. She looked at the Border collie. Jess was straining towards Paul, every sense alert. He looked up at Jenny and barked again. Jenny gasped. Of course. Jess could help.

'*We* can't do it, but Jess can,' Jenny declared. 'He can swim out with the reins. He's a strong swimmer.'

Ian was silent for a moment. 'But he's only a pup,' he said.

Jenny swallowed. 'We've got to try, Ian,' she said. 'Jess is our only hope.'

She bent and put the reins in Jess's mouth.

'Hold on to Mercury, Ian,' she said, then she turned to Jess. 'Take it to Paul,' she commanded. 'To Paul, Jess!'

Jess didn't hesitate. The little dog plunged into the river and struck out for Paul.

Ian held Mercury's head firmly as Jenny watched Jess trying to swim against the current. Time and again the strength of the water pushed him further downstream, away from Paul. Three times the little collie was washed towards the bank and three times he plunged in again. The last time he scrambled up and began to run towards them.

Tears were streaming down Jenny's face as she realised the little dog had no chance against the force of the river. 'It's all right, Jess,' she said, as the collie came running up to them. 'You did your best.'

Jess barely looked up as he raced past her, the reins still in his mouth. Further upstream he plunged once more into the water.

Jenny gasped as she saw what he was doing. 'Look!' she said to Ian. 'He's letting the current carry him down towards Paul.'

'Clever Jess,' said Ian. 'He's going to do it!'

Jenny watched, as Jess swam towards Paul, paddling desperately to keep his course. He was nearly there.

'*Now*, Ian!' Jenny said, stepping into the water.

'Hang on to Mercury,' Ian warned as he followed her.

Together they waded into the river as far as they dared. Jess had reached Paul. Jenny's heart seemed to stop as Paul's free hand came up and grabbed at the reins.

'Now the other hand, Paul,' she whispered under her breath. 'You'll need both hands.'

Ian and Jenny looked on, the water swirling round their legs, as Paul let go of the tree root. For a moment the water caught him, spinning him round as his other hand tightened still further on the reins. Then both hands were grasping the lifeline.

'Back, Mercury,' Ian urged. 'Steady now, boy.'

The big horse backed obediently towards the bank. Paul hung on but Jenny was watching Jess. The collie was trying desperately to swim beside Paul but he was already exhausted after his fight against the current. As Jenny watched, she saw the puppy beginning to lose the battle

against the force of the water.

'Jess!' she yelled, lunging forward.

Paul saw the panic on her face and let go of the reins with one hand. Jenny breathed a sigh of relief as he grabbed Jess's collar. But now Paul was in danger again. With only one hand on the reins and Jess's weight pulling him back, he wouldn't be able to hold on much longer.

'Hurry, Mercury,' Ian urged, his face set.

The horse took another step backwards and his hoof slipped on the stones beneath the water. Paul had to let go of Jess's collar to grasp the reins again with both hands and Jess spun round in the current. The young collie struggled furiously against the raging torrent, his head disappearing beneath the water as the force of it overcame him. He was being swept away!

'No!' cried Jenny, leaning as far as she dared towards the little dog, her hands desperately searching. Water filled her mouth and her eyes as she scrabbled blindly for Jess's body. 'Jess!' she called, her breath coming in great gasps.

She felt the force of the current dragging at her, but then her searching hands found a bundle of wet fur. Jess! With a sob of relief she somehow managed to grab Jess's collar, and his familiar black and white head emerged. A hand reached out and grabbed her.

'Hang on!' said Ian's voice. 'Nearly there.'

The next few moments were a confusion of noise and water and cold. Then Mercury was stepping back on to the bank, Paul still just managing to hang on to his reins.

Jenny lurched as Ian gave her a sharp pull on to the bank, after lifting Paul clear. She lay there for a moment, the water singing in her ears. Though more distant now, lightning still flashed and thunder rolled overhead.

Jenny felt a warm tongue licking her ear. 'Oh, Jess,' she gasped, cradling the little dog to her. 'You're safe.'

'We've got to get Paul back quickly, Jen,' Ian said.

Jenny looked up at the urgency in his voice. 'Of course,' she said, getting to her feet. 'He must be in shock after his experience.'

Ian nodded. 'He is,' he agreed. 'But there's more than that.'

Jenny's mouth went dry. She looked beyond

Ian to where Paul was lying on the grass. He was doubled up and clutching the lower part of his left leg. 'What is it?' she asked.

'I think he might have broken his ankle,' Ian replied. 'Can you give me a hand to lift him up on to Mercury? The sooner we get help, the better.'

9

They made their way slowly back to Windy Hill. Ian led Mercury, while Jenny rode with Paul, holding the injured little boy fast in the saddle. A tired Jess stayed at the big horse's side.

Jenny was shining her torch a little ahead of Ian, but it wasn't really necessary. Mercury knew the way back to the farm and his stable very well.

Paul was white with pain and exhaustion but

the little boy hadn't complained once, not even when they had lifted him up on to Mercury's back. Jenny had made a pad out of her jumper and placed it between Paul's foot and Mercury's flank, like a cushion, but even so, it wasn't an easy journey for him.

'I'm sorry I ran away, Jenny,' Paul whispered in Jenny's ear as they approached the farmhouse.

Jenny drew the torch back a little so that its glow illuminated her face and Paul could read her lips.

'Why *did* you run away?' she asked as he looked up at her.

Paul snuggled closer to her. 'I didn't want to go to hospital,' he burst out.

Jenny turned his face so that he was looking at her again. 'I'm sure your parents wouldn't force you to go if they knew how you felt,' she said. 'Have you told them?'

Paul nodded. 'They don't take any notice,' he replied. 'They just say nobody ever wants to go into hospital.'

'Have you told them *why* you're so worried?' Jenny persisted.

Paul bit his lip. 'Fiona says there's no point,' he told her. 'She says they'll just think I'm a scaredy-cat. She says the nurses and doctors won't like me. They'll think I'm making a fuss.'

Jenny's heart went out to the little boy. 'Lots of people like you, Paul,' she said gently. 'Think of all the people out looking for you. Your dad is really upset and your mum is worried sick. Fiona was crying because you were missing.'

Paul stared at her, surprise written on his face. 'Fiona?' he said wonderingly.

Jenny nodded. 'Then there's my dad and Matt, and Carrie and Ian, and loads of other people. And they all like you. And they're all worried about you.'

'They don't really like me,' said Paul. 'They just feel sorry for me.'

Jenny took a deep breath. 'Did Fiona tell you that?'

Paul nodded.

Jenny tried to control her anger. 'That just isn't true, Paul,' she said firmly. 'Jess likes you just for yourself – and so do I.'

'Do you?' asked Paul. 'Don't you feel sorry for me?'

Jenny thought for a moment. It was important to get this right – to tell Paul exactly how she felt. 'I feel sorry that you can't hear,' she said carefully. 'But I don't feel sorry for *you*. Why should I? You're bright and good fun, and popular – and very brave! You're a friend.'

'A friend,' said Paul slowly. He looked up and smiled at her.

Jenny smiled back. She felt Paul relax a little as he took in everything she had said. Far in the distance the thunder still rumbled but the storm was moving away, out to sea.

'Look,' said Jenny. 'There's Windy Hill. Everybody there likes you.'

Light spilled out from the door of the farm-house as they clattered into the yard and Mrs Grace came rushing out.

'You've found him!' she cried, her eyes on Paul. 'I've just got back from Dunraven. I was beginning to worry about you two. Where did you go?' The rain had eased off now but Mrs Grace took in their dirty, bedraggled appearance. 'Explanations later,' she went on. 'Let's get you inside. Hot showers all round while I phone your mother, Paul.'

'Paul has hurt his ankle, Aunt Ellen,' Ian said. 'It might be broken.'

Mrs Grace helped Ian and Jenny lift Paul gently down from Mercury's back. Paul winced as he slid from the saddle but he managed a smile. 'It was Jess who saved me,' he told Mrs Grace.

Mrs Grace smiled at him as she carried him into the farmhouse. 'You can tell me all about it later,' she said. 'Let's make you comfortable first and let your family know that you're safe.'

By the time Jenny came back from her shower, Paul was tucked up on the sofa in a pair of her pyjamas, under a mound of blankets. Mrs Grace had made a temporary splint to support Paul's ankle until they could get him to hospital. Jess, having been rubbed dry, was now curled up at Paul's side

'Mrs McLay is on her way,' said the house-keeper. 'She'll take Paul to Greybridge Hospital to get his ankle seen to. Mr McLay is still out looking for him but Mrs McLay says she'll try to get him on his mobile phone. Now, who wants a hot drink?'

Ian and Jenny had told Mrs Grace the whole story, but Jenny noticed that the housekeeper hadn't asked Paul any questions. The little boy was still rather pale.

At the sound of a vehicle pulling up in the yard, she looked at Paul, saying, 'That'll be your parents, Paul.'

Paul's eyes widened. 'Will they be angry with me?' he asked.

Jenny heard the sound of car doors slamming, then feet running across the farmyard. The door burst open and Mrs McLay stood there, her eyes going at once to Paul. 'Paul!' she cried, rushing to him.

Paul took one look at her then opened his arms and burst into tears. Anna McLay scooped her son into her arms, hugging him as if she would never let him go, burying her face in his hair.

Paul struggled and laughed a little. 'You're squashing me,' he said, looking up at his mother.

Jenny felt a smile spread over her face. Mrs McLay loosened her grip a little, but Paul still snuggled close to her.

Jenny looked at the door. Mr McLay and

Fiona were standing there. Mr McLay looked white and strained. His hair was standing on end and his legs were covered in mud to the knees. Fiona's face was pale with shock and she looked as if she had been crying again.

Jenny got up from the table and went to her. 'It's all right now, Fiona,' she said. 'Paul's safe.'

'It was my fault he ran away, wasn't it?' Fiona asked miserably.

Jenny looked at her. Until tonight, she had never seen the other girl so unsure of herself. Usually Fiona went around telling everybody what to do and bullying them. 'It's all over now,' she said. 'You didn't know this was going to happen.'

'But it's still my fault that he ran away and got hurt,' Fiona said brokenly, a tear sliding down her cheek. 'Paul will hate me now.'

Jenny looked at the little boy. 'I don't think he will,' she said. 'If you take back all the stories you told him.'

Fiona flushed a deep red. 'I will,' she said. 'I've told Mum and Dad it was my fault Paul was so scared of going into hospital. I've told them all about it.'

Jenny put a hand on Fiona's arm. 'That's a start then, isn't it?' she said. 'Paul won't hold it against you, not once he understands that you felt left out.'

For a moment the old anger flared in Fiona's eyes. Then she went even redder. 'You're right,' she said. 'I was jealous of all the attention Mum and Dad were giving to Paul. But I didn't want this to happen.'

'You weren't the only one to blame, lass,' Calum McLay said gruffly. 'I've been a bit hard on Paul too.'

Jenny looked up at him. He looked completely washed out, not at all his usual confident self.

Mrs Grace coughed. 'I'm sure the McLays would like to have a few minutes alone together,' she said. 'I think I hear the jeep.'

Jenny and Ian took the hint and went with Mrs Grace to meet Mr Miles and Matt. Jess trotted alongside.

'I hear you two found him,' Fraser Miles said, getting out of the jeep as Matt parked it in the yard.

Jenny and Ian launched into their story once more.

But then Fraser Miles's smile began to turn into a frown. 'You mean you took Mercury out in that storm?' he said. 'After I had expressly forbidden it? You did well to find Paul, Jenny, but that was foolhardy after what happened the other day.'

Jenny flushed. 'I was just so anxious to find out if Paul was there,' she explained. 'And, besides, the storm hadn't started when I left.'

'Was Mercury all right?' her father asked.

'Oh, Dad, he was wonderful,' Jenny said, smiling. 'He got a bit of a scare when he first heard the thunder but I talked to him – and Jess ran beside him. It was amazing. Mercury seemed to be listening to me. I just kept on talking to him and he settled down. Even when the storm was really close, even when the lightning was flashing all round the keep, he was all right. I think he's got over his fear. And we couldn't have saved Paul without him.'

Her father looked doubtful. 'He didn't bolt?' he asked.

Jenny shook her head. 'Truly, Dad, he was fine. He faced up to the storm and conquered his fear.'

'I rode him down to the river in the storm,' Ian put in. 'He was completely under control. And he was marvellous when we needed him to pull Paul out of the water. Really, Mr Miles, I think Jenny is right.'

'He's cured, Dad,' Jenny said. 'I know he is.'

Fraser Miles looked at his son. 'What do you think, Matt?' he asked.

'It certainly sounds like we should give Mercury another chance,' agreed Matt. Jenny heard the eagerness in her brother's voice.

'Well, I'm willing to,' said his father. 'It sounds as if Jenny and Jess might have done the trick.' Jess barked and he looked down at the little dog. 'So you're the hero of the hour again, Jess, are you?' he said, bending down to give the collie's ears a rub. 'Good boy!'

Jenny looked on as her father petted Jess. Jess's tail wagged so hard he nearly overbalanced!

The kitchen door opened then, and Calum McLay came out carrying his son tightly, followed by Anna McLay and Fiona. He nodded to them as he passed on his way to his vehicle.

Anna McLay came over. 'We can't thank you

all enough,' she said, her eyes filling again, with tears of relief. 'We're taking Paul to Casualty in Greybridge now.'

Jenny bit her lip. 'I know he has to go to hospital to have his ankle treated,' she said. 'But it was the thought of going to hospital that frightened him into running away. Do you think he'll be all right?'

Anna McLay smiled. 'I've explained to him that we're all going with him,' she said. 'And that I'll stay there with him if the hospital decide to keep him overnight.'

'What did he say?' asked Ian.

Mrs McLay laughed. 'He said he wanted to see the pictures of his insides.'

'Oh yes! They'll X-ray his ankle, won't they?' Jenny exclaimed.

Anna McLay nodded. 'He seems really interested in that. Who knows, maybe he'll change his mind about not liking hospitals.' She looked over at the Land Rover, where Calum McLay was hovering anxiously, making sure his son was comfortable on the back seat.

'It nearly took a tragedy to knock some sense into Calum,' Mrs McLay went on. 'But I think the message has got through. He realises what is really important now. And, if ever he looks like forgetting it, I'll be there to remind him. I'm not going to turn a blind eye to his bullying any longer. It's high time I stood up to my husband.'

'Good for you,' Fraser Miles said approvingly.

'And don't you worry any more about his plans to hound you out of Windy Hill, either, Fraser,' Anna McLay declared. 'After all, if it hadn't been for the people here, we might have lost Paul. There'll be no more dirty tricks if I've got anything to do with it. I'll see that Calum behaves himself.'

Matt laughed. 'I almost feel sorry for Calum,' he said.

'Don't be,' said Anna firmly. 'It's time he had a taste of his own medicine.'

'See you at school, Fiona,' Jenny said, walking with Mrs McLay over to the Land Rover.

Fiona looked at her. 'I suppose you'll tell everybody what I did,' she said.

Jenny shook her head. 'No, I won't,' she replied. 'I don't think you'll do anything like that again. That's all that matters.'

*

'Well,' said Mrs Grace as they watched the McLays drive off. 'It's good to see Anna McLay standing up to Calum at last. They'll both be better for it.'

'I agree, Ellen,' Fraser Miles said. 'He's got away with too much for too long.'

'Mr McLay and Fiona seemed much nicer tonight,' Jenny remarked, as they went back into the house. 'You know, I liked Mrs McLay before but I like her even more now. She must be brave to stand up to Mr McLay.'

'You can show courage, too, when something really important is at stake, Jenny,' Mrs Grace said. 'Look at the way you fought to save Jess when he was a pup.'

'Why don't you get Jenny on to Mr McLay over this lease business, Aunt Ellen?' Ian suggested.

Jenny sat up and Jess stirred and looked at her accusingly. 'I nearly forgot,' she said. 'I meant to talk to you about it, Dad, but then we heard that Paul was missing and it went right out of my mind.'

'What did?' asked Fraser.

'My idea,' said Jenny. She stopped, suddenly shy.

'Come on then, what is it?' encouraged Matt.

'Well,' said Jenny, 'I was wondering if Mrs Grace could come and live with us here at Windy Hill – and Ian too, of course,' she added.

Fraser Miles and Ellen Grace looked at each other.

'It's funny you should suggest that,' said her father. 'Ellen and I were thinking the same thing but we weren't sure if you would like it.'

'Like it?' shrieked Jenny. Jess jumped and shook himself. 'I'd love it!'

'Well then, that's settled,' said Mr Miles, smiling.

Jenny drew Jess towards her and gave him a cuddle. 'One big happy family,' she said, smiling at Ian.

Ian grinned. 'Except when Jenny and I fall out,' he added.

Jenny tossed her head. 'We won't fall out any more,' she declared. 'We're *friends*.'

10

Next morning Jenny answered a phone call from Anna McLay. Paul's ankle had been set and he was doing nicely.

'Did he like the pictures of his foot?' Jenny asked.

Anna McLay chuckled. 'The doctor gave him one of them to keep,' she told Jenny. 'He wants to pin it up on his bedroom wall.'

'That was nice of the doctor,' Jenny remarked.

Mrs McLay agreed. 'They're *all* nice,' she said. 'Paul is having a lovely time; meeting the other children and getting to know the nurses. In fact, when I told his doctor what had happened, and how worried Paul had become about not waking up again after his ear operation, he arranged for the doctor who will be in charge to come and visit Paul, to put his mind at rest. Keep your fingers crossed that it works, Jenny.'

'Oh, I will,' Jenny breathed. 'Mrs McLay, would it be all right if Ian and I came to visit Paul?'

'I was going to ask if you would,' Mrs McLay replied. 'Paul has been asking for you and for Jess.'

'Will we be allowed to bring Jess?' Jenny asked.

'The hospital has a pets policy,' Mrs McLay told her. 'They've discovered that the patients do much better if they're allowed to see their pets – especially the children.'

'Then we'll certainly bring Jess,' Jenny promised. 'Jess would *love* to see Paul!'

Mrs McLay told Jenny which ward to go to. 'There's a door at the end of the building that leads into the children's ward,' she said. 'It's lovely – and it has its own little garden outside. Paul will be so happy when he hears that Jess is coming to see him.'

Jenny rushed to tell Mrs Grace and Ian her news.

'I'll drive you over there tomorrow afternoon,' Ellen Grace promised. 'Anna and I can have a coffee and a chat and let the three of you have some time together.'

'Four,' Ian corrected her, smiling. 'Don't forget Jess.'

'As if I could,' said Mrs Grace as Jess scampered up to them at the sound of his name.

'You're going to see Paul tomorrow, Jess,' Jenny said, kneeling down and ruffling Jess's ears. 'Won't that be nice?'

Late that afternoon, the phone rang again and Ellen Grace picked it up. After a few minutes she called over to Jenny. 'Mr Palmer would like to speak with you,' she said, smiling.

Jenny was always delighted to speak to the vet who had helped Jess and Mercury get well. She dislodged Jess from her lap and went to the phone.

'It seems you've found a home for my abandoned puppy,' the vet said.

'Have I?' Jenny asked, confused.

'I've just had a phone call from Calum McLay,' Mr Palmer explained. 'Seems Pam Turner had told him about the pup, and that you'd said he might be perfect for Paul.'

Jenny's heart beat a little faster. 'So what did Mr McLay say?' she asked.

'He says if Paul wants the pup then he can have him,' the vet told her.

Jenny felt a wide smile spreading across her face. 'Oh, that's wonderful,' she breathed. 'Does Paul know, yet?'

'Not yet,' Mr Palmer replied. 'In fact, Mr and Mrs McLay thought you might like to tell him.'

'Oh, yes!' Jenny replied. 'Ian and I are going to see Paul tomorrow. He'll be so excited when he finds out.'

'Well,' Mr Palmer chuckled. 'I think we can do a little better than just telling Paul. We can *show* him! I've just had a word with Mrs Grace,' he explained. 'She's agreed to come and collect the pup on the way to the hospital tomorrow afternoon.'

'Wow!' Jenny said, excitedly. 'That would be fantastic!' Jenny put the phone down and turned to grin at Mrs Grace.

'I take it there will be *five* of you now,' the housekeeper said, smiling.

Jenny nodded happily. 'Ian,' she said. 'Guess what Mr Palmer's just told me!'

The following day, Mrs Grace turned the car into the hospital grounds and Jenny looked out of the side window eagerly. Beside her, Jess lifted his head and peered out of the window too. Ian was in the front seat with the puppy.

'Oh, no you don't,' Ian exclaimed, as the small brown bundle in his lap tried to wriggle out of his grasp. He held the puppy up so that he too could look out of the window.

Jenny smiled. The puppy was adorable, a honey-brown Border terrier with a scattering of darker brown on his back. 'Isn't he gorgeous?' she said.

'And full of life,' Mrs Grace laughed. 'Hold on to him, Ian.'

Mrs Grace parked the car and they made their way to the entrance at the end of the building. Both dogs were on leads. Mr Palmer had provided the puppy's collar and lead. 'A present for Paul,' he had said, smiling. 'Tell him to get well soon.'

A nurse in a white uniform came out of the entrance and looked at Jess. 'I'm Sister Joyce,' she said. 'I'll bet you've come to visit Paul. He's been talking all morning about it.' She looked at the Border terrier. 'I thought there was only one dog,' she said.

'This one is a surprise for Paul,' Ian told her, picking the puppy up. 'I hope you don't mind.'

Sister Joyce laughed. 'I don't mind,' she assured them. 'But it will take you a little while to get through the ward once the children see these two. Paul is out in the garden with his mum but you have to go through the ward to get there,' she said. 'Come on, I'll show you the way.'

They followed the nurse through the door and into the ward. Jenny looked around. The ward *was* lovely. There were bright posters on the walls and a play-area down at the end just in front of the French windows that opened on to the garden.

'Oh, look!' said one little girl, sitting up in bed. 'Puppies!'

Mrs Grace smiled. 'I think Sister Joyce is right,' she said. 'I'll just go and have a word with Anna and tell her you'll be along as soon as you can.'

Jenny looked around as children began to crowd round them. She couldn't just rush through the ward.

'What's that one's name?' asked a little boy in a wheelchair.

'Jess,' said Jenny, leading Jess across to him.

She looked at Ian. He was surrounded by children, all wanting to stroke the puppy. He grinned back. 'What a welcome!' he said.

'We find our pets policy works wonders with the children,' Sister Joyce said.

Jenny smiled. 'It certainly seems to,' she agreed. But there was one face she was looking forward to seeing more than any other – Paul's!

It was a full ten minutes before Jenny and Ian could drag themselves away from the young patients. Jenny put Jess down at the garden door and looked out over the lawn. Paul was sitting in a wheelchair with his mother and Mrs Grace on either side of him on garden chairs. He was chattering away, his face turned up to his mother's.

Jenny unclipped Jess's lead. 'Go and say hello to Paul,' she whispered in the young collie's ear.

Jess looked up at her, then he was off, racing down the garden. Paul turned as Jess came into view and opened his arms wide, his eyes shining, his whole face lighting up.

'Jess!' he cried.

Jess scampered up to him, his tail wagging furiously, and Paul bent to give him a cuddle. Jenny and Ian gave him a moment to welcome Jess.

'Now?' said Ian.

'Now,' Jenny agreed, and together they led the Border terrier pup down the garden.

Paul looked up as they approached. 'A puppy!' he cried. 'Oh, Ian, he's lovely. Is he yours?'

Ian grinned. 'No, he isn't mine, Paul,' he said.

Paul looked at Jenny, puzzled.

'He isn't mine either, Paul,' Jenny told him.

'He's yours – if you'd like him.'

Jenny watched as Paul's face changed from puzzlement to disbelief to joy.

'Mine?' he said. 'My puppy?' He looked at his mother.

'It's true,' she said. 'Dad told me all about it yesterday, but I didn't want to spoil Jenny and Ian's surprise by telling you. Do you like him?'

Paul bent down and stroked the puppy's head. The little dog looked up at him with deep brown, melting eyes. 'Oh, he's gorgeous,' Paul breathed. 'And he's mine! I'll take such good care of him.'

Jenny watched as Ian lifted the puppy to sit on Paul's lap. She was very sure that Paul *would* take good care of his pet.

'Can he come and visit me when I come into hospital next time?' Paul asked.

Jenny's breath caught in her throat. Paul had said 'when', not 'if'.

'So you're going to have the operation for your ears?' she asked him.

Paul nodded. 'I met Dr Tony, who will look after me while I am asleep during the operation. He's nice. He made me laugh. And

Dr Mike said I was very brave when I had my ankle set.'

'And so you were!' said his mother, smiling.

'Shall we go and have some coffee, Anna?' Mrs Grace suggested. 'We'll leave these five to enjoy themselves.'

Jenny watched as Ellen Grace and Anna McLay made their way back into the building. A young nurse passed the French windows and waved to Paul.

'That's Nurse Chrissie,' Paul said. 'She says I can have crutches soon – and Pippa is going to teach me how to use them.'

'Who's Pippa?' Ian asked.

'She's my friend,' Paul said. 'She's got a broken leg but she can get around really fast on her crutches. So can Jack. He's my friend too.'

'You seem to have made a lot of friends,' Jenny said, smiling.

Jess barked and the Border terrier leaped off Paul's lap and began to chase the young collie round the garden. Jess turned and waited for the smaller dog to catch up. The terrier butted Jess playfully on the nose and Jess crouched down and growled softly, batting a paw at the terrier. In a moment the pups were rolling over, playing with each other.

'Do you know what Carrie said about this puppy?' Jenny asked Paul.

Paul shook his head.

'Carrie said he was *meant* for you,' Jenny told him. 'And I think she was right.'

Paul giggled as he watched Jess and the Border terrier chase each other. 'They're going to be friends,' he said delightedly.

Jenny nodded vigorously. 'Just like us,' she said.

Paul beamed.

'What are you going to call him?' Ian asked.

Paul looked at the brown bundle of energy. The puppy broke away from Jess and came running up to Paul. The little boy bent and scooped him up in his arms. 'Toby,' he said. 'I'm going to call him Toby.' He bent his head to bury his nose in the puppy's soft fur.

Jenny and Ian looked at each other over the little boy's head.

'I think the puppy is a success,' Ian said, his eyes twinkling.

'You *could* say that,' Jenny agreed, as Mrs

Grace and Anna McLay appeared.

Jess barked and Jenny looked down at him. 'You've got a playmate. Jess,' she said. She looked at Mrs McLay. 'Can Paul bring Toby to visit Jess?' she asked.

'Toby?' said Mrs McLay, looking at the puppy. 'He certainly can. I'll make sure of it. I can't think of a nicer playmate for Toby than Jess.'

Jenny smiled. 'I can't think of a nicer playmate for *anybody* than Jess,' she declared.